MURDER

AT THE CARAVAN

Mystery fiction from the west coast of Ireland

DAVID PEARSON

THE BOOK FOLKS

Paperback edition published by

The Book Folks

London, 2023

This book is a work of fiction. Names, characters, businesses, organizations, places and events are either the product of the author's imagination or are used fictitiously. Any resemblance to actual persons, living or dead, events or locales is entirely coincidental. The spelling is British English.

ISBN 978-1-80462-096-0

www.thebookfolks.com

MURDER AT THE CARAVAN *is the fifteenth standalone mystery in The Galway Homicides series. Details about the other titles can be found at the back of this book.*

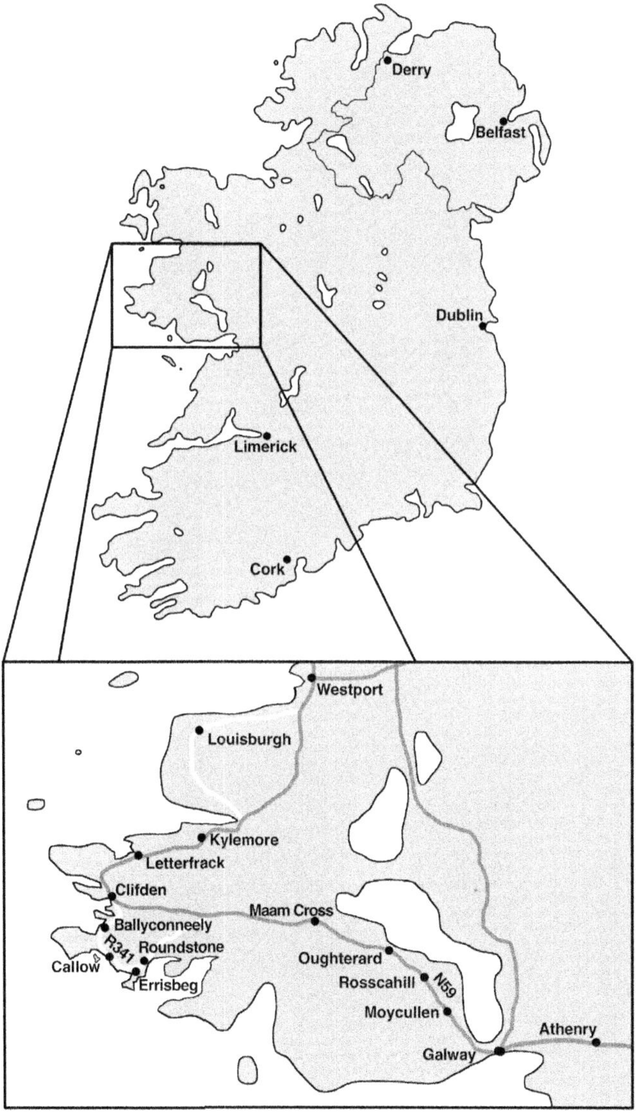
Derry
Belfast
Dublin
Limerick
Cork
Westport
Louisburgh
Kylemore
Letterfrack
Clifden
Maam Cross
Ballyconneely
R341
Roundstone
Callow
Errisbeg
Oughterard
Rosscahill
N59
Moycullen
Athenry
Galway

Chapter One

Christmas was a relatively quiet time in Clifden, on the west coast of Ireland. The shops and traders were busy, of course, but the population of the town was nothing like it was in the summer months. All of the holiday homes that surrounded the town were more or less deserted, with just one or two occupied by families who were keen to avoid the festive season in their normal habitat.

For Sergeant Séan Mulholland, a confirmed bachelor, it was a lonely time. The Garda station that he ran as Member in Charge would be closed on Christmas Day and the following day, with only matters of the most urgent nature being addressed by means of a notice fixed to the dark blue door of the premises, giving a contact number for a rota of officers who remained on call. Mulholland had a brother who lived in the USA, but both of his younger sisters had tragically died some years ago, so to all intents and purposes he was alone in the world – a situation that he rarely dwelt upon.

But this year, a colleague had invited Mulholland to spend Christmas Day with himself and his family. Garda Jim Dolan lived in a small development of houses known as The Spires. The houses had been built in 2000 and were sought after, as they enjoyed a good aspect to the rear, overlooking the sports grounds of the local Gaelic Athletic Association, and were close to the village and its amenities, which suited Dolan well.

Mulholland had selected a small array of Christmas gifts for his hosts. He had purchased a very cute and cuddly teddy bear for Jim Dolan's youngest girl, Aoife, who was just six years old, and a One4all token for his other child, Cormac, who was now nearly twelve. For their parents, he had selected books. Knowing Dolan's wife's interest in history, he had chosen a book describing the history of Connemara from the time of Grace O'Malley to the present day, and for Dolan, he had chosen a history of the Gaelic Athletic Association, which was one of his pet interests. The ladies in the well-stocked Clifden bookshop had wrapped the books beautifully in Christmas paper, Mulholland himself totally lacking this particular skill.

The invitation to dinner was for two o'clock, so Mulholland got up at nine in the morning, as was his habit, and had a light breakfast in anticipation of the feast to come, then went for a walk in the unusually mild and benign weather for the time of year. His bungalow on the Sky Road afforded magnificent views out to the west, and there was no traffic to speak of on Christmas morning as he strolled along the carriageway, taking in the fresh air and the sound of the curlews with their distinctive cry. Although he had lived in the place for virtually all of his working life, he still marvelled at the raw beauty of the area, with its rocky fields and sparse grass – more reeds and moss than anything else – stretching down to the constant motion of the sea below.

At half past one, he placed the Christmas gifts into the back seat of his old black Saab and set off for Dolan's house, arriving not ten minutes later.

When he rang the doorbell of Jim Dolan's house, he was greeted by Angela, his wife, who had Aoife clinging to her legs, curious to see who their visitor was. Angela

Dolan was a pretty, if not beautiful, woman in her late thirties. She had a shock of shiny reddish-brown hair that extended to below her shoulders, and a gentle oval face with high cheekbones and eyes that could be greenish or brown, depending on the light. She stood at around five feet seven inches tall, and was sporting well-cut trousers and a red, highly patterned Christmas jumper.

"Good morning, Sergeant, nice to see you. Happy Christmas to you," Angela said, leaning forward to gently press her cheek to his.

Mulholland, slightly embarrassed by the warmth of the welcome, and not entirely sure how to respond, said, "Yes, Happy Christmas to you all." He held out the bag containing the presents he had brought, giving it to Angela.

"Come on in. Jim is just taking the turkey out of the oven."

As they entered the kitchen-diner that spanned the entire back of the house, Mulholland remarked on the glorious view that the place afforded, and greeted his colleague.

"Morning, Séan. Come in. Take the weight off. Angela, will you get Séan a drink?"

"Would you like a sherry, Séan?" Angela said, feeling slightly uncomfortable with the use of the man's first name.

"Thank you. That would be lovely," Mulholland replied, although in truth, he wasn't really a sherry sort of person.

The meal went swimmingly. The food was plentiful, hot, and delicious, and the conversation flowed freely, helped by the wine which flowed equally freely. The two children were very well behaved, and kept the adults amused with the occasional inappropriate interjection. Aoife had already named her new toy 'Séan' in honour of its donor, and had said that her new 'Séan' was going to be her police bear who would chase all the bad people away and keep daddy safe.

By five o'clock, everyone was full of turkey and ham with all the trimmings. The main meal had been rounded off with plum pudding accompanied with whipped cream and brandy butter, the conversation was running thin, and Mulholland thanked his hosts profusely for a wonderful day, and took his leave. On his way out the door, Jim Dolan presented his boss with a bottle of vintage Irish whiskey, boxed, and beautifully wrapped.

It was dark when Séan Mulholland arrived back at his property. The westerly wind had got up, and was carrying salty air in off the Atlantic Ocean. The rain wouldn't be far behind. The moon was dodging in and out between fast moving clouds, giving a slightly sinister air to the night. Somewhere on the property a door was banging in the stiff breeze. He had forgotten to leave a light on, and the place looked desolate and sad as he made his way to the front door with its cracked and peeling paint.

Once inside, he put a match to the fire in the sitting room, and settled down to watch television. After a few minutes the bright orange flames from the turf and the sweet characteristic smell of the burning peat permeated the room, Séan Mulholland, in mellow form, dozed off.

He didn't know how long he had been asleep, but the shrill jangle of his house phone penetrated his slumber, and brought him somewhat foggily back to reality. He picked up the phone, rubbing his face with his spare hand.

"Mulholland," he said into the device.

"Oh, Sergeant, thank God, I've got you. I was ringing earlier but there was no reply. This is Christine Dalton here. I'm calling about my brother. I don't know where he is, and I'm worried sick."

"Sorry, Christine, can you tell me a bit more? What's your brother's full name, to begin with?"

"Oh, yes, sorry. His name is Gerard McCarthy. Dalton is my married name."

"And what has you worried about him, Christine?" Mulholland said.

"He was supposed to be here today. I invited him for Christmas dinner, but he never turned up, and I can't reach him on his phone. It just keeps going to voicemail. That's not like him at all. I hope nothing has happened to him."

"Well, look, Mrs Dalton, we're not supposed to do anything about this sort of thing until the person has been missing for forty-eight hours or more. You'd be amazed how many folks just turn up with a perfectly sensible explanation of why they weren't where they were expected to be. And to be fair, there's not much we can do about it at this time on Christmas Day. But if you give me Mr McCarthy's address, I'll see if we can have a look at it tomorrow for you. How does that sound?"

"Is that the best you can do, Sergeant? I was hoping you might be able to start investigating this evening."

"Have you been to wherever he lives to see if he's there, by any chance?" Mulholland said.

"No, not yet. I've been up to my eyes with Christmas dinner and all sorts. My sister's three small children are here, and we can't just walk out and leave them."

"Right so. Give me his address then, and I'll get someone to go around in the morning. I'm sure he'll just have fallen asleep or something," Mulholland said, beginning to lose patience with the woman.

"He lives in a mobile home over near Kingstown, off the Sky Road. He's bought a site there and he has planning permission for a bungalow, so while he's getting that built, he's staying in the temporary arrangement. But the place has an Eircode. I can text it to you."

"Yes, please, Christine." Mulholland reeled off his personal mobile phone number.

"Thanks, Sergeant. Won't you let me know immediately if you find anything out?"

"Yes, of course. Just send me the location straight away now. I'll talk to you tomorrow."

Chapter Two

When the call was over, Séan Mulholland went back into the sitting room. The fire had subsided quite a bit, and there was just a pile of glowing embers in the grate, but it was giving out a fair bit of heat still. He sat back down in his armchair, and tried to pick up whatever drama was playing out on the television, but he couldn't settle to it.

"Damn it! I'd better go out as far as Kingstown and see if this fella is in, or I'll get no peace. Bloody nuisance. I'll give him a good earful when I find him, that's for sure," he said to himself. He placed the wire mesh fireguard in front of the hearth and, this time, left a light on in the room to welcome him on his return. Thankfully, he had kept a clear head, so he put on his outdoor coat and collected his powerful hand lamp from the hall stand.

The lights on the old Saab weren't the best, and if there was a moon, it was well hidden behind heavy clouds, so Mulholland drove slowly as he didn't want to end up in the ditch. At least he was able to use Google Maps on his smartphone clipped into a mount attached to the windscreen. The Eircode he had been given was quite a bit beyond Kingstown, on out to a plot of high ground overlooking Eyrephort Beach. Mulholland spotted the mobile home that Christine Dalton had described, positioned quite a bit inside a large grassy field. He parked his car in the entrance and got out, bringing his powerful lamp with him. The gate was already open, but Mulholland could see no light on in the mobile home. He went to the door of the large pale green temporary dwelling, and rapped three times on the glass, but there was no response. He tried the door, but it was locked, and in any case, he didn't want to enter the place without just cause.

Mulholland noticed that there didn't appear to be any curtains on the windows, so he mooched around till he found something to stand on, climbed up on it, a little unsteadily, and shone his lamp in through the window. The lamp did a fine job of illuminating the interior of the place, but there was no sign of life inside. The home was reasonably tidy, the only sign of inhabitation being a half-full milk bottle on the table beside a box of cereal and an empty bowl. Apart from that, it looked well-kept and comfortable.

Mulholland went around to the other side of the caravan where he assumed the bedroom to be located and repeated his examination. This time there were curtains on the window, but they were drawn back so he could easily see inside to a double bed, which was neatly made; a nightstand with a lamp and an alarm clock; a few pairs of shoes and a wardrobe with the door hanging open displaying a number of outfits on hangers.

When Mulholland had finished looking inside the caravan, he shone the torch all around the area, but there was no sign of anything untoward. A stiff breeze was circulating all around him, and he had a desire to get back to the shelter of his vehicle as quickly as he could. Nevertheless, he walked up over the rough grass to where a large concrete slab had been constructed, alongside which was a sizeable stack of concrete blocks, awaiting the rest of the building materials that would create Gerard McCarthy's new house. He turned around, and even in the darkness he could see that the aspect of the new dwelling would provide superb views out over Eyrephort Beach, and Inishturk Island beyond. Happy now that the missing man was not at home, Mulholland retraced his steps, turned his car around, and drove back the way he had come.

* * *

St Stephen's Day was a little depressing for a lone bachelor, but Mulholland was not too badly affected. He spent a lot of time alone, and he was generally reasonably content with his own company. There would be good sport on the television today, in any case, to keep him amused. He enjoyed watching horse racing, but hadn't yet mastered the skill of placing bets online, which was probably just as well. Indeed, the man didn't have a computer to his name at home, even though broadband was now readily available all over the region.

He rose at ten o'clock, and cooked himself a light breakfast. He was still somewhat full from the feasting of the previous day at Jim Dolan's house. By eleven o'clock he was feeling a little restless. The racing on TV wouldn't start for another couple of hours, and there were no newspapers published on that day, so he decided to give Christine Dalton a call to see if her errant brother, Gerard, had made contact.

Christine Dalton answered the phone almost before it had started ringing. She must have been standing by the instrument anxiously, hoping for news from her brother.

"Hello, Christine. It's Sergeant Mulholland here. I'm just calling to see if you've heard from your brother at all?"

"Hello, Sergeant. No. Nothing, and I'm fierce worried now. Did you find anything out yourself?" the woman said.

"No, I'm afraid not. I went out to the site at Kingstown and had a bit of a poke around last night, but there was nothing. The caravan was empty, and there was no sign of a vehicle anywhere. What sort of car does Gerard drive, anyway?"

"He has a sort of truck thing. He uses it to haul building materials to the site. It's quite new. I think it's Japanese."

"And what colour is it, Christine?"

"'tis mostly white, when it's not covered in mud."

"And would you have the registration number of it at all?"

"No, I'm sorry, Sergeant. I have no idea."

"Well never mind. We can find that out ourselves. Look, Christine, I'm going to set a few things in motion. It's very strange that he hasn't been in touch with you all right. There's not a whole lot doing in the force today, but by tomorrow we'll be back to full strength and we can get organized properly. But listen, you let me know the instant you hear from him, whatever the circumstances, won't you?"

"I will, of course. And thanks, Sergeant."

Mulholland wasn't entirely sure what things he could set in motion on the day after Christmas, but he did feel the need to do something. Maybe he would forego the racing and go back out to Kingstown himself and have another look around in the daylight. He wondered if he should bring another officer with him, but decided not to disturb their peace for the moment.

On the drive out along the Sky Road towards Kingstown, Mulholland pondered the situation. He knew he should try and get inside the mobile home that Gerard McCarthy was living in, but he didn't want to just break into it. Firstly, he didn't really have due cause, as the official procedure called it, and secondly, he didn't want to leave the place open to the four winds and vulnerable to vandalism, although he felt there was only a slim chance of such an outcome, given where the dwelling was located.

He pulled the old Saab in where the lorries delivering building materials had created muddy ruts in the soft ground at the edge of the road adjacent to the site. In the daylight, he could now see the extent of the plot. The foundations of the house had been built on the highest point, where the property would enjoy a splendid view down the hill, to the beach and sea beyond. At the road, a thick hedge of gorse and brambles with copious nettles growing up through the shrubs marked the boundary.

Mulholland got out of his car and walked up the hill to where the mobile home was sited, quite close to the large concrete slab upon which McCarthy's bungalow would soon be constructed. He went to the door, where six solid nine-inch breeze blocks had been arranged in makeshift steps, with three piled on top of each other against the door, then two in front of that and one on the ground furthest from the unit. Mulholland examined the door, and the area around it carefully. There were a few brown streaks on the wall of the mobile home to the left of the door, and a splash, about the size of a large coin, on the lowest of the three steps. The splash had a sort of star shape, as if a liquid had been dropped from a metre or so above the concrete.

"Probable cause, here we go," Mulholland said to himself. He walked back down to the boot of his car, where he had a variety of tools stored. He selected an iron bar with a flat piece at one end and a hook at the other, formed with a V-shaped split.

"That should do the job nicely," he said to himself, weighing the implement in his right hand as he closed the car up again.

Back at the mobile home, he inserted the straight end of his crowbar into the gap between the door and the frame, close to the lock, and pushed the bar back towards the body of the caravan. After two attempts, the lock sprung, and the door swung open, hitting Mulholland on the chest and causing him to stagger backwards. But he managed to stay more or less upright and quickly regained his balance.

He stepped up into the temporary dwelling. As he had seen the previous night, the inside of the unit was in good order. The table was clear, except for the half-full bottle of milk which hadn't moved, and the cushions on the long sofa that hugged two of the outside walls of the mobile home were neatly placed. The cooking rings were closed up, and the area was clean and tidy. Mulholland walked down the short corridor to the rear and went into the bedroom that filled one end of the mobile home completely. The room contained a double bed, nicely made up; a wardrobe; a small locker beside the bed, and the window had two sets of curtains – one net curtain closest to the glass, and one of patterned cotton that matched the carpet and the duvet cover. Mulholland looked in the wardrobe. Inside there were three business suits, two sports jackets, several pairs of trousers, and a shelf containing an array of shirts, socks and underwear stored in a tidy fashion.

The last room to be investigated was the small bathroom that contained a portable toilet, a wash hand basin that folded up against the wall to save space when it was not in use, and a shower cubicle, which although small, had everything that was needed for a decent wash. There was a small, mirrored cabinet containing shaving foam, a razor, a roll-on deodorant, a hairbrush, and a small bottle of expensive aftershave.

Mulholland could see no sign of any altercation within the four walls, nor was there any sign of Gerard McCarthy. It was as if the man had just vanished into thin air.

Mulholland left the caravan. He tied the door closed with a short piece of orange nylon string that he found nearby, and walked the full extent of the site, but could see no sign of anything to alarm him.

Chapter Three

On 27 December, things were returning to something like normal in Clifden. Many of the offices remained closed until early January, but the shops were open again and the Garda station was fully manned.

When Mulholland arrived at the station, after he had brewed the first mug of tea for the day, he placed a phone call to Christine Dalton. Just as before, the woman answered the call on the first ring.

"Good morning, Christine, it's Séan Mulholland here. I'm just calling to see if you've heard anything from Gerard?"

"No, Sergeant, not a whisper. It's really not like him at all. I'm sure something has happened to him. Can you not do something?"

The woman was obviously very distressed, and Mulholland was beginning to believe her that something serious was amiss.

"What does Gerard work at, Christine?"

"I'm not sure of the details, Sergeant. He does things with computers. I don't understand any of that stuff. I usually glaze over when he's talking about work, to be honest."

"Does he have an office somewhere, Christine?"

"He told me he has some sort of a place in Galway. I think it's in Dominick Street over one of the restaurants, but I've never been there."

"Have you contacted any of his friends, Christine?"

"Sure, of course I have. There's a lad called Todd that he's known since he was a teenager, but he hasn't seen him either. And there was a girl he was seeing, Amanda her name is. But they haven't been together for a few months. I didn't much like her anyway, although I only met her the once."

"Right. Well, I'm going to get a few of the lads out to Kingstown to have a proper look around the site. I'll put out a message about his truck too once we get the registration number. Try not to worry, Christine. These things nearly always work out in the end. I'm sure he'll turn up."

"Thanks, Sergeant, I hope so."

When the call was over, Séan Mulholland invited Jim Dolan and Peadar Tobin into the office at the back of Clifden Garda station.

"Right, men. Can you take a few of the uniformed lads on out to Kingstown where this chap Gerard McCarthy was living. I was out there yesterday, and I think I may have seen a few blood spatters on the side of his mobile home, but I can't be sure, and anyway they could be old. But I get the feeling there's something amiss all the same. Search the hedges and all around and see if you can find anything of interest."

The two Gardaí acknowledged Mulholland's request, gathered a small team of uniformed officers armed with stout sticks, and set off out west. Mulholland, now more or less on his own manning the station, put a call through to Roundstone, and spoke to Garda Mary Fallon.

"Hello, Mary. Did you have a good Christmas?"

"Hello, Sergeant. Yes, thanks. What about yourself?"

"Ah, it was grand, thanks. Listen, I'd like you to do something for me. I need a registration number for a vehicle owned by a man called Gerard McCarthy with an address in Kingstown out near Inishturk. Although I think he may have an address in Dominick Street in Galway as well, so it could be registered there. I don't know my way around the computer, but you should be able to sort it out for me."

"That's no problem. Will I call you back when I have it?" Fallon said.

"Yes, but I want you to put out a national alert for the vehicle too when you get the registration number. The owner has gone missing, and his sister is going spare with worry. It's not a stop-and-detain. Just make sure we find out where the man is if the vehicle is located. Is that all clear?" Mulholland said.

"Yes, understood, Sergeant. Is there anything else?"

"No, that's it for now. Thanks, Mary."

Mulholland returned to the dregs of his tea, which had now gone cold, looked at it disdainfully, and decided it was time for a fresh brew. When he was seated again with a new drink, he started to think through what they knew about the missing man. So far, there was no evidence of foul play. But Mulholland had to admit that it was a bit odd, all the same. Most people don't just not turn up to family Christmas dinners, and the fact that he had gone more or less off the air too was worrying. Mulholland toyed with the idea of calling the matter in to the Galway detectives, but thought better of it.

He decided to wait and see what Dolan and Tobin turned up out at Kingstown, if anything, and then determine whether to call in the cavalry or not.

* * *

Jim Dolan took the lead when the team arrived at the site in Kingstown.

"OK, you two, start walking the perimeter. Beat down the gorse and nettles all along the ditches, and collect anything at all that you find in an evidence bag. It doesn't matter how insignificant it might seem, bag it. I'm going to focus on the mobile home. Peadar, will you oversee the lads out here?"

"Yes, Jim, no problem."

Dolan walked across to where the large two-tone green mobile home was positioned. He undid the orange nylon string that Mulholland had used to secure the place the previous night, donned blue vinyl gloves, and went in. The unit was divided into three main areas. At the front, looking out over the incredible view, seating was arranged all around the walls in a U-shape. The seats were covered in patterned velour which was a kind of browny-grey colour, with pink flowers embroidered into the fabric.

The middle section of the caravan housed the kitchen with a three-burner gas hob, a stainless-steel sink, and a grill, beneath which was a small fridge that could be powered either by gas or electricity, or even a battery if neither of the other two energy sources were available. Beyond that, the corridor narrowed to make room for the small shower room on the left, and a full-length wardrobe on the right, before opening up again to accommodate two bedrooms, one with a double bed and the other with two bunk beds.

Dolan started at the front. He removed all of the seat cushions and piled them up on the table in the centre of the 'U', and started to lift the plywood covers off each of the under-seat storage boxes.

In the first one, he found footwear. There was a pair of wellington boots, size 10, a pair of sturdy black leather work boots, also size 10, and a pair of flat ladies' pumps, size 4. Dolan looked inside each item of footwear in case there was anything hidden in them, but there was nothing.

The next box along held just two board games. *Monopoly*, the UK version, and *Scrabble*. Both of the cardboard boxes containing the games were play worn, but otherwise unremarkable. Dolan lifted the lid on each in turn, but found them to contain only exactly what you would expect.

Dolan continued to search the rest of the place with the same thoroughness. He found little of interest, except that in the base of the wardrobe, there was a cardboard box, and in it were a number of office-like files, each labelled with a plastic tag, suspended laterally across the sides. He scanned the labels briefly. Several were just what you would imagine a well-organized person to have. They were labelled 'Bank', 'Tax', 'Insurance', 'Car', and so on. But at the back, the labels were different. They seemed to refer to clients, as they had the names of companies and individuals on their labels. These files had more documents than the others too.

Dolan didn't know whether it would be in order to remove the box, or any of the individual files, so he just photographed them with his phone, capturing as much detail as he could with the rather basic camera. He was just retuning the box to its original position, when a shout went up outside.

"Over here. I've found something," the young Garda called out.

Dolan went to investigate.

Chapter Four

The 'something' that the young Garda had discovered was the body of a man. It was hidden well back in the dense undergrowth of weeds and gorse bushes down near the entrance to the site. The body was fully clothed, but even lying as it was in a very awkward position, it was clear that the man had been beaten about the head and face. It was also perfectly obvious that he was dead.

"Bloody hell, Ronan. Are you OK?" Dolan said when he arrived beside the young Garda.

"Yes thanks, I'm fine. Better than yer man, in any case. He's almost unrecognizable," Ronan said.

"Right, well, stand well clear now. Don't let's contaminate the scene any more than we need to. I have some tape in the boot of my car. Would you go and get it and close off the whole area around here? I'd better call this in."

Jim Dolan walked out onto the road, and was pleased to see that there was a decent phone signal. He called the station in Clifden. Mulholland answered, and Dolan told the sergeant what had been found.

"Dear God, Jim, that's terrible. You're sure he's dead?"

"I'm no pathologist, Sergeant, but there's not really any doubt. It looks like some of the animals out here have been at the body too. It's not much, but I've seen that before. It's not pretty."

"Right. Well, you stay there to secure the site. Send Peadar back in with Ronan. Is he OK?"

"I think he may have lost his breakfast, but apart from that, he's grand."

"Good. I'll get onto Galway now, straight away. Thanks, Jim."

* * *

Senior Detective Inspector Maureen Lyons was enjoying the short break. She had taken an extra day off along with her partner, Superintendent Mick Hays, and the plan was that they would go into Galway around lunchtime, hit the sales that had just broken out in the shops, and get something to eat later on when they were all shopped out.

On Christmas Day, Hays and herself had spent a very enjoyable time with Lyons' sister, Sheila, and her family out at the old farm close to Athenry. Since Sheila's husband, Séamus, had had a heart attack two years earlier, they had sold much of the farmland, retaining just ten acres around their house. Séamus, an industrious man who didn't relish giving up farming completely, had purchased a few Connemara ponies with the intention of breeding them. They required little maintenance, and were very hardy, so they more or less looked after themselves most of the time.

When Lyons' phone started to ring at just before noon, she hoped that whoever it was calling wouldn't upset their plans.

"Hello, Maureen. It's Séan here out in Clifden."

Although Maureen Lyons outranked Séan Mulholland, they still called each other by their first names, unless there was some formal occasion. Lyons had worked with

Mulholland when they were of equal rank, and they had remained close colleagues, despite Lyons' somewhat meteoric ascent to senior detective inspector.

"Oh, hello, Séan. Compliments of the season to you," Lyons said.

"Same to you and Mick, Maureen. Listen, we have a bit of a situation out here that needs a senior officer. Are you available?"

"Go on, Séan," she said with a sigh, looking at Mick Hays and rolling her eyes to heaven.

Mulholland went on to describe the discovery of the dead man out on the Sky Road, and the reports of a missing Gerard McCarthy called in by his sister.

"Do you think it's him, Séan?"

"Very likely, but we have made no attempt to identify the body yet. I thought it best to call you first."

"Great. Thanks a bunch. OK. Well, I'd better get things organized then. We'll need the pathologist, forensics, and the undertakers out too. Have you enough manpower to secure the scene for the moment, Séan?"

"Ah, yes, no problem. There's two or three of them still out there with Jim. I'll tell them you're on your way."

"OK, Séan. Thanks for letting me know. Can you send me the address of the location, I'll be in touch."

"Yes. It has an Eircode. McCarthy is building a house on the site, and I suppose he needed it for deliveries. It's on its way. Thanks, Maureen."

* * *

Dr Julian Dodd was at home in his spacious detached house close to Oranbeg just outside Galway. Dodd was five feet seven in height, and although he could be a bit pompous in his demeanour, he was nevertheless an excellent pathologist. Dodd had been very helpful to the Galway detectives in solving some of their most challenging cases, and although he often complained at being called out to some desolate location where a body had been found, in the dark, and sometimes in heavy rain, he was always thorough and professional in his dealings.

He was just pouring himself and his wife a glass of pre-luncheon oloroso sherry when his phone rang.

"Dodd," he said into the instrument, a little sharply.

"Good morning, Doctor, it's Inspector Lyons. I trust you had a pleasant Christmas?"

"Which, I have no doubt, you are about to bring to a shuddering halt, Inspector."

"Sorry, Doc. We have a dead body in a ditch out near Kingstown, west of Clifden. It looks as if he may have been beaten to death. Do you think you could attend?"

"Naturally, dear woman, though it's not at all convenient. Where is this godforsaken place?"

"I'll send you the Eircode and you can put it into your sat nav. Are you able to leave soon, Doctor? It will be getting dark at about quarter to five."

"I'll leave as soon as I have the location, Inspector, and may I ask you to refrain from speculation as to the cause of death until I have examined the body?"

"Great. Thanks, Doc. I'm heading out to the scene myself. I'll see you there."

Dodd hung up without saying another word. Lyons made a face at the phone. "One of these days…" she said out loud to no one in particular.

"I guess that's our shopping trip out the window then, hun?" Hays said.

"Sorry, Mick. That was Séan and Dodd in that order. They've found a body out in Kingstown. I'll have to go out. I might grab one of the others to go with me too. Will you be OK?"

"Yeah, no problem. I might go down to the sailing club and see if there's anyone around. Give me a bell later and we'll see what gives."

Hays was an avid sailor, and enjoyed taking the sloop that Lyons had bought for him as a surprise gift, using a bonus she had been awarded by the Gardaí, out on Galway

Bay. But at this time of year, the boat was out of the water for the winter, but still, the social aspects of his hobby continued unabated.

"OK. Thanks, Mick." Lyons gave her partner a quick kiss, grabbed her weatherproof jacket, her keys and handbag, and left the house.

When Lyons got underway, she decided that she would like to have another one of her team along with her. It was always better to have four eyes in these situations, and as the location of the incident was quite remote from her station in the centre of Galway, she could do with the extra support. She used the hands-free system in her car to call Mill Street. She recognized the voice of the man who answered the call.

"Hello, Danny, it's Inspector Lyons. Do you know if Eamon Flynn or Sally Fahy are in just now?"

"Good morning, Inspector. Inspector Flynn is away out to Taylor's Hill since early on. There's been a break-in at one of the hotels over the holiday when it was closed, and a lot of valuable stuff has been stolen, it seems. But I think Detective Sergeant Fahy is upstairs. Would you like me to put you through?"

"Yes, please, Danny."

There were a few clicks and beeps from the phone before Sally Fahy answered.

"Detective unit," she said.

"Hi, Sally. It's Maureen Lyons. How are things there? Much going on?"

"Oh, hello, boss. It's fairly quiet. Inspector Flynn is away to investigate a robbery at one of the hotels, but there's nothing much else doing. Did you have a good break?"

"Yes, thanks. But listen, I'm afraid I'm on my way out to Clifden. It looks like a man has been killed out on the Sky Road near Kingstown. Séan Mulholland was onto me a while back. I'd like you to come out if you can. I may need a hand," Lyons said.

"Oh, right. God, that's awful. Was he hit by a car, or something?"

"I'm not sure of the details yet, Sally, but we'll know soon enough."

"Aren't you supposed to be on a day off too?"

"Never mind. I'll get the day back at some stage. But listen, if I text you the co-ordinates, are you in a position to leave pretty soon?"

"Yes, no problem. Do you need anything brought out?" Fahy said.

"Maybe you could grab a decent camera. But that's about it. And leave a message for Eamon. Just give me a minute or two to send the text. I'll have to pull in."

"OK. I'll get going anyway. Is Dr Dodd going to attend?" Fahy said.

"Yes, he's on his way, rather grumpily, I'm afraid."

"No change there then. OK. See you soon."

Lyons pulled in when she was just past Moycullen where the road widened out. The land hereabouts provided good pasture, and cattle grazed in the fields on both sides of the road. She sent the reported location of the killing to Fahy. It was a cold, overcast day, with the temperature gauge on Lyons' Volvo indicating just six degrees Celsius. Due to the Gulf Stream that brought warm waters up from the Gulf of Mexico to wash around the west coast of Ireland, it rarely went below freezing in Galway. Wind and rain were more familiar visitors to the county as the low-pressure weather systems blew in from the south-west, dumping the water that they had collected crossing the Atlantic Ocean on the land. But today, although the rain was probably not very far away, it hadn't actually started to fall.

Chapter Five

Lyons pressed on with the drive. Even in the somewhat gloomy conditions, once she had passed Oughterard the rugged scenery lifted her spirits. As the road rose up out of the town, the landscape changed. Now she was travelling through bogland, peppered here and there with small lakes. The road undulated, and the verges provided a meagre ration of short grass that was eagerly grazed by sheep that roamed freely on the roadside. The sacrifice of losing her day off didn't seem so bad after all, now that she was out in the wilds of Connemara. Her only regret was that she didn't have her partner with her, and that she was going to yet another unexplained death.

When she reached Clifden, she stopped at the large supermarket close to the monument at Seaview, at the start of the Sky Road. She went in and bought a pre-packed sandwich and a cup of freshly brewed coffee. She paid using her bank card, and went back out to the car to consume her snack. Ten minutes later she hopped out of the car to dispose of the sandwich wrapper and empty paper cup, and brushed herself down on the footpath to get rid of any stray crumbs.

Back in the car, she started it, and turned the heater up a notch to compensate for the lower temperature that always seemed to pervade the air in Clifden. As she passed the entrance to the Abbeyglen Castle Hotel, she saw headlights flashing her from behind, and recognized Sally Fahy in her brightly coloured Hyundai squad car. Lyons waved, and the two vehicles continued in convoy out towards Kingstown Bay.

When they arrived at the location, things were slowly taking shape. Dr Julian Dodd hadn't arrived yet, but Mulholland had instructed his men wisely, and the area where the body was found was well cordoned off. A couple of uniformed Gardaí were in attendance making sure that only authorized personnel gained access to the body, and keeping the very low traffic volumes moving on the road adjacent to the site.

Lyons and Fahy got out of their vehicles. Lyons showed her warrant card to the officer at the entrance to the building site, and he lifted the blue and white tape for Fahy and herself to pass underneath. When Dolan saw the two women arriving, he came across to meet them.

"Hello, Inspector; Sergeant. Thanks for coming out," he said.

"Afternoon, Jim. What's the story here?" Lyons asked.

Dolan told Lyons the very few details that they had at this stage.

"Do we know who the victim is, Jim?"

"Not formally, but it's probably Gerard McCarthy. He was living in that thing over there while he was waiting for his house to be built," Dolan said, gesturing towards the mobile home.

"Have we searched it properly?" Lyons said.

"I've had a quick look, but we've been focused on the body."

Lyons turned to Sally Fahy.

"OK, Sally. Can you go and give the caravan a good going-over. Bag anything you think might be relevant. You know, laptop, correspondence, mobile phone, you know the drill."

"Right, boss," Fahy said. She walked off towards the mobile home.

Lyons resumed her conversation with Jim Dolan.

"Did you have an OK Christmas, Jim?"

"Yes, we did, thanks. We invited Sergeant Mulholland over for Christmas dinner. I think he enjoyed the company, and the kids found him good fun. What about you?"

"It was grand. Mick and I went across to Athenry to my sister's place. I could have done without this today, though. Oi oi, here comes Dodd, and Sinéad Loughran too, if I'm not mistaken."

Sinéad Loughran was a forensic scientist in her thirties. She was pretty, with longish blonde hair that she normally wore in a ponytail during working hours. She was tall and slim, but her most abiding characteristic was her incurable good humour. No matter how gruesome the scene, at any time of day or night, Sinéad Loughran always seemed to be in good form. But underneath her attractive, cheerful exterior, she was fastidious and talented in her work, often discovering salient evidence from the flimsiest of clues. Lyons was always pleased to see her arriving at a crime scene.

A uniformed Garda out on the road directed the ever-increasing fleet of official vehicles into some sort of order. Dodd got out of his shiny black Lexus and went to the rear of the car. He opened the boot and exchanged his stout black brogues for green wellington boots, and retrieved his old Gladstone bag before making his way into the field. He greeted Lyons in the customary manner.

"Where is my subject then, Inspector? Let's not delay any more than necessary."

Lyons and Dolan showed the doctor to where the body was lying largely hidden in amongst the undergrowth.

When he saw the position of the body, he turned to Loughran.

"Sinéad, can you get a tent and some stepping plates here. Any chance we have of finding any evidence will be long gone with all these people milling around."

Loughran did as she was asked, and within minutes a white plastic tent and a number of bright yellow stepping plates had been put in place. When this had been accomplished, Dodd advanced on the deceased. The doctor spent quite a few minutes bent down over the body. He looked carefully at the position of the limbs and examined the man's hands. Then he moved up to the head, and brought out a small, illuminated magnifying glass to study the corpse in detail. Eventually he stood up, packed his few implements back into the old leather bag, and left the tent.

Lyons approached when she saw him emerging.

"Yes, I know, I know, Inspector. What did he die of and when did it happen? Well, I would say he died from a severe beating around the head with a blunt object. His face is almost destroyed, and I'd wager his skull has been fractured if not worse. As to when, I'd estimate somewhere between three and four days ago, but I might be able to narrow that down a bit when we get him back. Discover what the bugs tell us. Do you know who he is yet?"

"We think it may be a Gerard McCarthy, but we aren't sure. Is it OK to move the body now? I'd like to see if he has any ID on his person, such as a wallet or driving licence."

"Yes, of course, be my guest. I'll hardly get to the post-mortem today. Let's say ten o'clock tomorrow."

"Right. I'll see you there."

Dodd went back onto the road, changed his boots back to shoes and departed.

When he had gone, Lyons gave the word that the body could be moved. A solemn black van had arrived at the location, and two burly men brought a body bag made of thick black plastic into the tent where the body was resting. They lifted the man, and expertly folded his limbs into something like their original position, then placed the corpse into the body bag, zipped it up, and carried it to their vehicle.

One of the uniformed officers who had been overseeing the exercise inside the tent bent down to where the body had been lying and picked something up from the flattened ground. He went outside in search of a senior officer.

He found Lyons talking to Sally Fahy who had returned from her search of the mobile home.

"Excuse me, Inspector, but I found this under where he was lying," the young man said, holding up a piece of narrow green ribbon from which dangled a single key.

"Thanks, Guard. It looks like it might be the key to the caravan. Here, put it in this evidence bag," Lyons said, holding out a small paper bag with a see-through window.

"So, what did you find up beyond?" Lyons said to Fahy, nodding towards the caravan.

"Nothing of interest really. I grabbed a box of files that were in the wardrobe, but that's about it. I suppose we should let Sinéad loose on it, you know, fingerprints, boot prints, all that sort of stuff."

"Yes. Maybe you'd go and have a word? Ask her to look out for a weapon too. Dodd said he'd been beaten badly with something blunt, so maybe a stout stick or a bit of pipe. She knows what to watch out for."

"What are you going to do, boss?"

"I'm going back into Clifden. I want to talk to Séan Mulholland, and then I'm heading back to town. Tomorrow, first thing, can you start digging on Gerard McCarthy? Go through those files with a fine-tooth comb. All the usual stuff – bank details, phone records, known associates, social media, the lot. Let's try and find out who wanted him dead."

Chapter Six

Darkness was setting in early as Lyons drove back along the Sky Road towards Clifden. There was no sign of the magnificent orange sunset that could so often be seen out over the ocean, west of the road. Instead, the greyness just seemed to be intensifying over the bleak hills, reflecting Lyons' mood as she drove eastwards.

When she arrived in the town twenty minutes later, the streets were more or less deserted, reflecting the general gloom brought on by the weather and the after-Christmas hangover. Lyons parked her Volvo outside the Garda station and went in. She found Séan Mulholland in the office to the rear of the premises, nursing a mug of tea. The office had an open fire, and although the place could do with a lick of paint and a bit of a refresh, the fire gave the room a cosy feel with the sweet smell of burning peat adding to the atmosphere.

"Hi, Séan. I don't suppose there's another one of those left in the pot?" she said as she opened her jacket to get the benefit of the fire, and sat down on the other side of the table.

"Of course, Maureen. I'll get it for you now."

Mulholland got up and went to fetch a mug of tea for Maureen Lyons. When he returned, he had a saucer with several chocolate biscuits with him too.

"Thanks, Séan. The air out there certainly gives you an appetite."

"What's the story out beyond?" Mulholland said as Lyons tucked into the snack and took the first mouthful of tea, both of her hands gripping the blue and white striped mug for heat.

"It's not good, Séan. Yer man must have been lying there for a couple of days. Didn't the sister say he was expected on Christmas Day and never turned up?"

"Aye, she did that. So, maybe he was killed on Christmas Eve. God, that's awful. Sure, wasn't I out there myself and never saw the poor man? Mind you, it was pitch dark at the time," Mulholland said.

"Yes, and he was well hidden in the gorse too. You'd never have found him at night. Will you go and tell his sister?"

"Yes, I'll drive out there when we close up here. She'll be very distressed, poor woman."

"Do we know if he had any other next of kin? Was he married or anything?" Lyons said.

"I don't think so, but I'll find out when I'm at the house."

"Right, oh and can you ask if Gerard had any distinguishing marks on his body, like a tattoo or a birthmark, or even an appendix scar?"

"Crikey, Maureen, is he that badly beaten?"

"I'm afraid so. His face is all but destroyed."

* * *

Christine Dalton lived in a relatively modern bungalow in a townland known as Shanakeever. The translation of the name from Gaelic means 'old neighbour' which is hard to account for, but doesn't take away from the natural beauty of the location. But although the place had a rugged beauty, the land was poor, and the only enterprise that it sustained was the husbanding of a few sheep, meaning that to make a living, those that lived in the area had to seek work away from home.

Dalton's house overlooks Shanakeever Lough, and if you follow the narrow road on for another 500 metres, you come to a larger lake, Lough Auna. The road terminates at an ancient burial ground with a megalithic tomb, though the place is rarely visited, being very remote and difficult to find, and in any case, wildly overgrown.

Séan Mulholland had seen Maureen Lyons off on her way back to Galway before getting into his Saab and setting out for the Daltons'. He drove along the main Westport Road until he came to the sharp left-hand corner where the Shanakeever Road branched off to the right. He proceeded out past the quarry and the caravan park, before taking another right turn at the fork in the road, leading him on towards the lake. When he arrived at Dalton's bungalow, he turned in, and drove up the steep tarmac driveway to the front of the house. The wind had got up now, and the rain had just started. It was light enough, but Mulholland knew that in fifteen or twenty minutes there would be an unrelenting downpour. Fitting weather to accompany the sad news that he had to impart, he thought to himself.

Making sure that the handbrake on his old car was pulled well up to prevent it rolling down the steeply inclined driveway, he got out. He donned his peaked cap, stepped up to the doorway and rang the bell. He heard the noise going off deep inside the property, and after a short wait, he saw the shape of someone approaching through the glass panel in the upper half of the front door. A moment later, Christine Dalton opened it.

Mulholland touched the peak of his Garda cap.

"Good evening, Christine. May I come in?"

"Of course, Sergeant," she said. She stepped aside to allow Mulholland to enter.

"Go on down the back to the kitchen. I'm just about to make my tea. Can I get you a cup, or maybe a sandwich?"

"No, thanks, you're grand, Christine. I just came to have a word."

The two of them went to the back of the house. Dalton's kitchen had a look of the 1970s about it. Kitchen units in a pale beige colour with dark oak trim adorned three of the walls, with a washing machine incorporated close to the stainless-steel sink. More storage was provided by overhead cupboards, and Mulholland noticed that one of the doors was hanging off the carcass a little where the top hinge had given up. The cooker was a free-standing white number with four solid black rings and an eye level grill, the top edge of which was heavily scorched through use. A bare wooden table sat in the centre of the room, surrounded by four wooden rail-backed chairs. The floor was covered in rather tired linoleum, in an abstract orange, green, and brown pattern.

"Sit down there, Sergeant, and take the weight off. Are you sure I can't get you a drink of something?" Christine Dalton said.

"No thanks. But you'd better sit down too, Christine. I'm afraid I have bad news."

"Oh, no, don't say that, Sergeant. Is it Gerard?" Christine Dalton said, tearing up.

"We have discovered the body of a young man out at the site in Kingstown, Christine. Now, we aren't absolutely sure it's your brother, but it may well be. How old was Gerard, Christine?"

"Let's see. He was born in 1991, so that would make him thirty-two this year. Yes, that's right, he's thirty-two."

"Can you tell me, Christine, did Gerard have any distinguishing features, like a birthmark, or a scar that you're aware of?"

Christine Dalton cried freely. She retrieved a handkerchief from her apron pocket and dabbed her eyes and her runny nose. Mulholland waited for her to steady up somewhat.

"Can't we tell by looking at him who he is, Sergeant?"

"The man we've found has been disfigured quite badly, Christine. It may not be easy to tell from his face."

Christine Dalton sobbed loudly, calling the name of her brother into her handkerchief in a muffled voice. After another few minutes of heartfelt sobs, she composed herself a little.

"Well, he did break his arm when he was a teenager. The left one, I think. Yes, it was his left arm. He came off a bicycle on the road and he had to go to hospital and have it set back. But he was very brave about it."

"Kids, eh! Tell me, Christine, was Gerard married at all?"

"No, he wasn't. He had a few girlfriends from time to time, and we met some of them, but he never tied the knot. I told him he was too fussy, but it never made any difference."

"What about close friends or business acquaintances?" Mulholland said.

"I don't know, Sergeant. Gerard was quite a private person."

"What sort of business was he involved in, Christine?"

"God, I don't know much about it. Something to do with computers. But I don't understand such things, and if he told me, it just went in one ear and out the other."

"Right. Well, maybe I could come and collect you tomorrow morning and we could go into Galway? We'll have to ask you to identify the man, Christine. I'll need to be here early. Would eight o'clock be agreeable?"

"Heavens, I suppose so."

"And can I get someone to come over and stay with you, Christine? I know it's an awful blow for you."

"Ah, no, Sergeant. I'm well used to being on my own since my husband died a few years back. I'll be fine, but thanks."

"Right, so. Well, I'd better be getting back to the station. Can we say around eight tomorrow then?"

"Yes, OK."

Séan Mulholland left Christine Dalton to her dark thoughts. He felt for the woman. He knew she had a sister, but he had a feeling that she didn't live locally, but he couldn't recall exactly where she was from.

Chapter Seven

It was coming up to half past six when Lyons hit the evening traffic on the outskirts of Galway city. The rain that Mulholland had predicted had caught up with her, and it made for a miserable end to her journey. She had the car's heater and air-conditioning going full blast to keep the windows free of mist, but even so, visibility was poor. Lyons decided not to go back to the Garda station, but to go home instead. She'd had enough for the day, and tomorrow would be a busy one, trying to get to the bottom of why Gerard McCarthy had been killed, and by whom.

When Lyons got indoors, the house was warm and welcoming. Hays had arrived home sometime previously, and was sitting in the front room watching some inane quiz show on television. He turned it off as soon as he saw Lyons.

"Hi, love, come in. Can I get you some tea or something to eat?" Hays said.

"No, thanks, Mick. I'm full of tea, and Séan stuffed me with chocolate biscuits too, so I don't need anything. How did you get on?"

"Grand. There were a few of the lads down at the club and we had a good old chat. Yer man, Tommy McKeever, got a new Avon dinghy for Christmas and he said it took three delivery drivers to get it into his garage. Bloody thing was massive!"

"Somebody loves him, then!" Lyons said.

"Anyway, what about you? What's the story in the wild west?"

Lyons told her partner what had transpired out at Kingstown.

"Gerard McCarthy. Hmm… I'm sure that name rings a bell somewhere, but I can't place him. I'll have a root around tomorrow in work and see if anything pops up. Any idea what line of business he was in?" Hays said.

"No. But Séan has gone out to see his sister, so we'll know more in the morning. Now, Superintendent, enough about work for today. I'm all in," Lyons said. She sat down on the sofa beside her partner and snuggled up close as he turned the TV back on.

* * *

The following day, the Garda station at Mill Street was returning to something like business-as-usual following Christmas. The coloured paper garlands that had been hung from the ceiling by way of seasonal decorations looked a little sad and out of place, but the small plastic Christmas tree with its myriad of flashing, coloured lights that had been put in the front window overlooking the street was still fully operational and provided a modicum of cheer to the otherwise rather sombre atmosphere.

When Lyons arrived at work, she called Sally Fahy and Eamon Flynn into her office.

"OK, folks. We need to get busy. I have to go over to the mortuary for the post-mortem at ten o'clock. So, I'd like you to get started. Sally, can you hook up with John O'Connor? Get into all the social media sites you can find, and see what information we can collect on Gerard

McCarthy. Get John to scour Facebook, Instagram, LinkedIn, Twitter and even TikTok. Eamon, can you get onto the banks? Sally may get his account details from the box of files she brought in. Then talk to Revenue and the other government agencies and see what they have on the man. By the time I get back, I'd like to have a full profile of Gerard McCarthy. OK?"

"Yes, boss. Let's get to it," Eamon Flynn said to Fahy. They got up and left the office.

* * *

Séan Mulholland collected Christine Dalton at the appointed hour. When they had set out for the city, Mulholland said, "How are you bearing up, Christine?"

"This is dreadful, Sergeant. I didn't sleep a wink. I've been trying to figure out why anyone would want to target Gerard. It doesn't make any sense to me at all."

"I know, Christine. But have no fear, the detectives in Galway are a good crew. They'll get to the bottom of it, don't you worry. Inspector Lyons is a tough woman. She's cracked some very difficult cases in her time. You might meet her inside when we get there."

"God, I hope so, Sergeant. I'll have no peace till we find out what's gone on."

The two settled into an easy silence as Mulholland drove along toward the city, both lost in their own private thoughts.

When they arrived at the mortuary at the back of Galway University Hospital, Mulholland escorted Christine Dalton inside. He left her in the waiting room and went off to liaise with the pathologist to set up the identification.

Dr Dodd's assistant wheeled the metal gurney into position so that the body could be viewed through the window that looked out onto the corridor. The corpse was covered from head to toe in a plain green cloth, and the assistant stood by to reveal the head, which had been made as presentable as possible, given the serious injuries the young man had suffered. When it was all set up, Mulholland went out and collected Christine Dalton. They walked down to the end of the corridor, and Mulholland knocked twice on the glass. A curtain was drawn back, and then the green cloth covering the body was pulled back to reveal the man's face.

Christine Dalton stared in at the lifeless body, and put her hand to her face.

"Oh my God," she exclaimed, but said nothing more.

A seemingly endless silence followed which Mulholland was reluctant to break, but eventually, he felt it was getting awkward.

"Sorry, Christine. Could you just confirm for us?"

"That's not my brother, Sergeant." The woman turned and buried her face in Mulholland's chest, sobbing loudly.

Mulholland didn't know what to do, but he was not a man that was easily fazed. When Christine Dalton had composed herself a little, Mulholland asked her, "Are you sure, Christine?"

Mrs Dalton just nodded, and said, "Yes, I'm sure. I know the man is right messed up, but it's not Gerard, of that I am certain."

"God, Christine, I don't know whether to be happy or sad for you. But I'm very sorry. We just assumed it was him because of where he was found, and the key that we found under the body. And, of course, you said that Gerard hadn't turned up for Christmas dinner. I'm really sorry. Look, let's get out of here."

Mulholland continued to support his charge as they made their way back out along the long corridor. As they emerged into the open area inside the door of the mortuary, Maureen Lyons was coming in.

Lyons went towards the woman, extending her hand.

"I'm very sorry–"

Mulholland interrupted Lyons before she could complete the sentence.

"We need to have a little chat with you, Inspector. All three of us. Could we go somewhere and get a cup of tea or something?" He was shaking his head from side to side and frowning at Lyons. She got the message.

The three of them walked in silence to the front door of the main hospital, and went in. Lyons led them to the cafeteria that was positioned down along the main corridor to the wards. The facility wasn't crowded at that early hour, but the staff had the place up and running all the same. The smell of freshly brewed coffee and toast filled the air. Mulholland and Dalton sat down at a four-seater table, and Lyons went off to get a large pot of tea, cups, milk, sugar and spoons.

A few minutes later, Lyons returned carrying a tray, and set down its contents on the table. She placed the empty tray on a vacant, adjacent table, and took her seat. Without being asked, she poured three cups of tea for them, and waited for one of the others to speak.

"Christine Dalton has informed us, Inspector, that the body in the morgue is not that of her brother, Gerard."

Lyons took a sip of tea.

"Heavens, Mrs Dalton, I'm really sorry to have put you through this. That's dreadful. You must have got a terrible fright. I hope you can understand why we believed it was Gerard."

"Yes, of course, Inspector. But it isn't, and that leaves us with another mystery, doesn't it? Where the hell is he?"

Chapter Eight

Maureen Lyons drove back around to Mill Street and parked in the yard at the back of the Garda station. Mulholland had left with Christine Dalton for the journey back to Clifden, leaving Lyons with a jumble of conflicting thoughts running through her head. When she got inside, she summoned Sally Fahy, Eamon Flynn and John O'Connor to her office.

"Now, before any of you tell me anything, I have some news. The body that was found out at Kingstown is not that of Gerard McCarthy, or at least that's what his sister tells us."

The other three looked at each other in surprise. Flynn was the first to speak.

"Cripes, boss. What does that mean?"

"It means, Eamon, we have two problems. Firstly, we need to identify the dead man as a matter of priority. So, please get going on all the usual stuff – missing persons, fingerprints, and anything else you can think of. And the dead man must have had a vehicle too. Kingstown isn't exactly accessible by any other means, so where is his car, or whatever? Secondly, Gerard McCarthy is missing, and we must assume that he is also a person of interest to us.

So, all the good work you have all done to find out about him is still very relevant. What have you got?" Lyons said.

Sally Fahy was first to speak.

"John and I did a good trawl of the web, boss. We got hits on LinkedIn and Facebook, but none of the other social media sites. He apparently is the boss of a company called GMC-IT. We got an email address and a phone number for him, oh, and a photograph, but that's about it," Fahy said.

"Did you call the number?" Lyons said.

"Eh, no, boss. We thought he was lying dead in the morgue, so there wasn't much point."

"OK. Well, that's the first job. And do it from a landline here so it's recorded, and John, when Sally is making the call, see if you can trace his location."

"Right, boss," O'Connor said. The young Garda liked nothing more than to get stuck into some detective work using electronic devices of any kind.

"Now, what do we know of GMC-IT?"

After a moment of slightly awkward silence, Flynn spoke up.

"We'll get onto it straight away, boss."

"Sally, what else was there on LinkedIn? You know the way they put up associates and links to other people that do business with the subject, all that stuff."

"Nothing, boss. No associates. No links. Sorry."

"Damn. What about banks, mobile phone providers, and the rest of it?"

"We'll get on it as soon as we're finished here, boss," Flynn said a little defensively.

"Yes, please. I'm going to call Séan and see if he can go back out to Kingstown and have a look for a car that may have belonged to the deceased. Meantime, can someone call Roundstone? Séan tells me he put Mary Fallon on the case to try and get a reg number for McCarthy's vehicle," Lyons said.

"Do you want stop-and-detain, boss?" Fahy asked.

"Yes please. Don't have him arrested, just helping with enquiries, but go easy on Fallon, she may have already set it all up. Right then, off you all go. Let's check in around lunchtime and see what we've got. Oh, and circulate the photograph from LinkedIn too."

When the team had gone off to get to work, Lyons called Séan Mulholland.

"Good morning, Séan. How did you get on with Mrs Dalton afterwards?"

"Oh, hello, Maureen. God, she was in a fierce state altogether. I had to go into the house with her and get her a whiskey to try and settle her. Have you found out anything more?"

"We're just getting started here, Séan. But listen, when you were out at Kingstown, did you spot any vehicles around and about that looked out of place?"

"No, I can't say that I did, Maureen. And there was no sign of Gerard's truck either. What are you thinking?"

"Well, whoever it is that was found in the undergrowth must have got there by car. And as he clearly didn't drive it away, and Gerard seems to have run off in his own machine, then there must be another one somewhere about. Can you send Jim out to have a good snoop around and see if he can locate it?"

"Jim is away over at Leenaun. Some fella reckons a dozen or so of his sheep have been taken. They're probably on the butcher's block by now. I'd better go myself. I'll head out there now in about twenty minutes and I'll give you a call if I find anything. I don't suppose you have any idea what I'm looking for? Like, is it a car, or a van or what?" Mulholland said.

"Sorry, Séan, I haven't a clue."

"Right. I'll talk to you later. Bye."

Lyons was pretty certain Séan Mulholland was going to fortify himself with a nice big mug of tea and a few chocolate digestive biscuits before he set off, and she wasn't wrong.

* * *

"Sally, look at this," John O'Connor said. He gestured for her to come across to his PC.

"What have you got, John?" she said, sitting down beside him.

"See here. I found this in a back edition of the *Connacht Tribune*. Or should I say, Google found it. Looks like there's some kind of hook-up between the university and McCarthy's company."

O'Connor pointed to the screen where an article from the newspaper was displayed. It showed a photograph of Gerard McCarthy shaking hands with a Professor Rían Madden, head of IT, and a caption that read 'University College Galway assists local businessman with new data mining project'. The article went on to say how the university's powerful computers were to be rented out at night to McCarthy for large volumes of data processing. 'Our systems are largely dormant between about midnight and six in the morning, so it's terrific that a local firm can make use of all that power that would otherwise go to waste, and the contribution Mr McCarthy will make will help us to purchase new equipment for the student body,' Madden had said.

"What sort of computers do they have at the university, John?" Fahy said.

"Well, when I was there, they had hundreds of PCs and servers of course. But they also have a beast of a mainframe. I think some of the government departments use it too. I knew one of the operators quite well, and she showed me around it a few times, although, to be honest, there wasn't a lot to see. Not like the old IBM systems like the 370."

"What this one called?"

"It's an IBM z series. I think it's a z12. Ursula told me that IBM sold it to them at a very favourable price, and they gave them buckets of software with it too. I used it a few times for my degree. It was unbelievably powerful."

"How do you measure the power of those things?"

"There's a technical term for it, it might be MIPS or something, but all I know is that it can crunch a few million transactions a minute. Ideal for data mining," O'Connor said.

"What exactly is data mining?" Fahy said.

"It's to do with analysing and categorizing huge volumes of data. Say when you buy something on Amazon. Well, as much of your personal data that they can harvest is stored alongside your purchase. Now just imagine how many sales Amazon make worldwide in a day, and how much data they accumulate as a result. Well, data mining is all about analysing that data, and breaking it down into segments that are useful to advertisers. That's how you get prompted by Amazon next time you go on their site for something related to previous purchases. It's called 'next best offer', and lots of people make a further purchase based on it, and so on."

"Crikey, John. You never know what's really going on, do you?"

O'Connor smiled.

"OK, that's only the start of it. Think about how much data eBay, Facebook, Instagram, Google and all the others amass. Billions of items of data every day. And someone like McCarthy is mining it all so that they can make even more money out of their subscribers. People think social media is a service that they get for free, but just look at how wealthy these companies have become. It's crazy."

"I see what you mean. Anyway, I wonder if your friend Ursula would be willing to have a chat with us?" Fahy said.

"I'd say she'd be cool with that. She's very nice. Would you like me to give her a call?"

"Yes, would you? But we don't want to put her in an awkward spot, so if she doesn't want to, that's fine too."

"OK. I'll call her later."

Chapter Nine

Séan Mulholland, suitably refreshed, got into his old Saab and set off for Kingstown once again. It was a bright, clear morning as he navigated the Lower Sky Road, but in the distance, out to the west, he could see clouds from the next Atlantic weather front mustering. He calculated that by nightfall the weather would have changed for the worse. As he drove along the quiet road, he passed a couple of old-timers walking slowly supported by stout hawthorn sticks. They would be out checking on the few sheep they kept to supplement their state pension. Mulholland saluted them as he drove past carefully, and they responded in the same manner, as was the custom in rural Ireland.

He parked at the roadside just at the entrance to the building site where Gerard McCarthy's new home was to be constructed. There was no sign of any workmen, but Mulholland wasn't surprised by this. Most tradespeople would be taking this week off in any case, with a view to restarting work in the first few days of January.

When he got out of his car, he reached into the back seat and fetched his heavy navy-blue Garda overcoat and put it on. It was still cold, and the stiff westerly breeze was reducing the temperature even further.

Locking the car, he set off walking back the way he had come. He calculated that if someone had been calling on McCarthy, and was hoping to spring a surprise on the man, such a person would most likely stop their vehicle before the site, and walk the rest of the way.

Mulholland looked in every field, but could see no sign of a car. He walked almost half a mile in his quest, searching on the sea side of the road as he walked away from his car, and examining the inland area on the way back. There was no traffic of any kind on the road as he walked along, and the silence was only punctuated by the sound of the wind rustling through the hedgerows, and the occasional call of a curlew or seagulls in the distance.

He got back to where his car was parked. Feeling as if he was on a bit of a wild goose chase, he set off using the same pattern walking away from the site in the other direction. When he had gone almost as far as he thought sensible, he came to a cottage set well back from the road. The little house was in a poor state of repair. It had, at one time, been whitewashed, but the salt-laden rain that blew in from the sea had acted like sandpaper on the paintwork, and it was now just a streaky mess. There was a pair of rusty wrought-iron gates at the entrance to the steep, overgrown gravel path leading up to the front door, but they too had fallen victim to the corrosive elements, and were rusted through, hanging off their hinges.

Mulholland looked up at the property and saw a thin plume of blue smoke issuing from the one and only chimney, so he decided to call in to ask if the occupant had seen anything out of kilter on the day the young man found in the field had lost his life.

Having rapped three times on the flimsy front door, its paintwork once having been a dark green but now cracked and peeling, he waited patiently on the step, admiring the view out to sea. After quite an interval, the door was opened, and a wizened old man appeared, dressed in a filthy brown two-piece suit and a collarless striped shirt.

"Sorry to disturb you, Mr eh…?"

"Cloherty, Paddy Cloherty, Sergeant."

"Mr Cloherty, I'm investigating an incident that took place near here on Christmas Eve, we think. A young man was attacked and badly beaten on the site where a new house is to be constructed. I was wondering if you had seen or heard anything out of the ordinary that night?"

"Let me see now," the man said, scratching his bristly chin, "Christmas Eve, was it? Well, I was away into Clifden early on to collect my money. Then I had a couple of pints down at the Bridge Tavern. I got home about six, and fell asleep in front of the fire."

"And what about later on, Mr Cloherty?"

"Oh, wait a minute now. Yes, there was a caller. I wasn't expecting anyone, so I got a bit of a start."

"What time would this have been?"

"Let me see. Oh yes, I remember. The news was just starting on the television, so that would have been nine-ish. I missed the headlines when I went to answer the door."

"And who was your visitor?"

"Just some lad asking for directions to Gerard McCarthy's place. That's the man that's building the house, you know. So, I pointed him in the right direction, and he left. I was glad to be rid of him."

"Did you see what he was driving, at all?"

"No, I didn't. I don't pay much attention to that sort of thing, Sergeant, but I can tell you that he had someone with him. I could see into the car from here because the inside light was on. He had a young woman with him, in the driver's seat."

"Are you sure about that, Mr Cloherty?"

"I am. I know what I saw. I may be old, but my eyes are as good as yours, I can tell you!"

"Could you describe the man that came to the door?"

"Ah, not really. He was young, but he was only here for a minute or two, and he had a woolly hat on. That's all I can tell you."

Sensing that there was nothing more to be gained from questioning Paddy Cloherty further, Mulholland thanked the man, and left.

As Séan Mulholland walked away from the impoverished cottage, he wondered if a similar fate awaited him, when he eventually retired from the Gardaí. His own house needed doing up. Like Cloherty's, the paint was almost gone from the outside, and inside, he hadn't upgraded anything since he had moved in twenty-five years ago. He would need to do something about it, and soon.

On the way back to his car, as he passed the land some three fields back from McCarthy's and around a slight bend in the road, he saw an old Ford Cortina languishing at a jaunty angle on the inside of the ditch.

Retracing his steps, he found the entrance to the field, and went in. As soon as he got a good look at the old car, it was clear that it hadn't moved in some time, quite possibly a good few years. The glass was covered in green mildew, and all the tyres had perished and gone flat. The paint was faded and streaked, and it soon became obvious that this was not a car that had been used to transport the young man to his ultimate deadly encounter. Nevertheless, Mulholland took down the details in his notebook from the faded red rear number plate, and trudged back out onto the road through the damp grass.

When he got back to his car, he stood leaning against it and pulled his phone out of his inside pocket and called Maureen Lyons.

"Hi, Séan. What's the story?" Lyons said.

"Hello, Maureen. I'm out here at Kingstown just beside McCarthy's plot of land. I've had a good look around up and down the road in the fields and so on, but there's no sign of a car anywhere that the dead man could have used to get out here. But I did find an old-timer in a cottage that told me he had a caller on Christmas Eve around nine o'clock asking for directions to McCarthy's. What do you want me to do?"

"Damn. Are there any other houses or farms anywhere near there that you could call on to see if anyone else saw anything?"

"There're a few more places on out the road a bit, but I think they are mostly holiday cottages. They are probably empty. You'd hardly come all the way down here for your Christmas break, now, would you?" Mulholland said.

"All the same, Séan, for the sake of thoroughness have a look at them for me, will you? See if there's anyone else in. You never know, we might get lucky."

Mulholland sighed audibly into the phone.

"Fair enough, Maureen, but I'm not very hopeful. I'll let you know."

Lyons wanted to thank the man for his efforts, but he had already hung up.

Chapter Ten

While Séan Mulholland was exploring the territory out in the far western extremes of Connemara, Lyons was back in Mill Street with her team gathered around her.

"Right, folks. We now have not two but three distinct problems that need to be resolved as soon as possible, before the trail goes cold. Eamon, help me out here," Lyons said.

"Firstly, we know that the deceased is not Gerard McCarthy," Flynn said. "So, our first problem is, who is he? No ID on his person, apart from his clothing, which is run-of-the-mill Dunnes Stores for the most part, and no other way to identify him, apart from scouring the missing persons bulletins. Incidentally, no luck there for now either. Secondly, as Gerard McCarthy seems not to be dead, where is he? Again, no trace, and we have his vehicle registration now, and Mary Fallon has circulated it here and in the North. Thirdly, it seems from what Séan Mulholland has told us, that the dead man was delivered to meet his fate by someone. That ties in with the fact that there is no abandoned vehicle in the vicinity of the killing. The delivery driver, allegedly, is a woman, but we know nothing more about her or the car she was in, and it may not have been a female at all. The witness is an old guy who was looking out to the road from his front door, so he could have mistaken a man with longish hair for a woman. Does that sum it up for you, boss?"

"Yes, Eamon, it does. So, anyone got any ideas on how best to proceed?"

"Doesn't McCarthy have a place here in town? We need to get in there and see what's what," Fahy said.

"Good idea, Sally. Can you take that for us? It's supposed to be in Dominick Street over a restaurant, but then just about everything is all along there. See if you can find it and get in," Lyons said.

"Do I need a warrant?"

"Probably. But see if you can get in without breaking anything and you should be all right. I take it there was no reply when you rang GMC-IT's phone?"

"No, boss, it just rang out."

"And isn't there some tie-up with the university, boss?" Flynn said.

"Yes. John found a piece in the paper about it. Why don't you and I go out there and talk to Professor Whatsit. See what he can tell us about McCarthy's company. Give me a few minutes and then we'll set off," Lyons said.

"Right, boss. In the meantime, I'll see what more John O'Connor has been able to find out about McCarthy's company."

Lyons went to her office and called Superintendent Mick Hays.

"Hi, Mick, it's me. Remember you said that the name Gerard McCarthy rang a slight bell with you? Well, have you thought of where you heard the name before?"

"Hang on, I think there's something here on my computer."

Lyons could hear the click clack of Hays' keyboard before he came back to her.

"Yes, here it is. It looks like a marketing email from a company called GMC-IT. It's offering to supply lists of people who are interested in sailing boats. The email address is no-reply@gmc-it.com, so it's spam in a way, but it invites me to contact a Gerard McCarthy to take the matter further and gives a phone number."

"Cool. What's the number?"

Hays reeled off the number from the email that he had received.

"Thanks. Nice one," Lyons said.

"How's it going anyway?"

"It isn't. Look, I gotta dash. See you later."

"OK. Bye."

Lyons hung up and lifted the receiver immediately again. She dialled the number Hays had called out. The call was answered on the third ring.

'Hello. You have reached GMC-IT. There is no one available to take your call at the moment, but if you leave your name, number and a short message after the tone, we will return your call as soon as possible.'

As soon as the beep was played, another, more mechanical voice cut in, 'This voicemail box is full, and your message cannot be recorded. Please try again later.' Then the line went dead.

* * *

It only took Sally Fahy five minutes to walk around the corner into Dominick Street from the Garda station in Mill Street. Lyons was right. Much of the street, which is of mixed construction, was occupied by hostelries of various kinds, including a night club and several fashionable restaurants. Many of the old buildings were faced in stone, and stood proudly alongside the more contemporary premises that had been remodelled in bland, plastered concrete during the 1980s.

Fahy walked slowly down the street, looking up, above the ground floor units. Several of the upper floors appeared to be vacant, but when she got as far as O'Dea's Restaurant which occupied a spacious double-fronted lot, painted in dark grey, and offered sumptuous fare of all kinds, she noticed that overhead there was a large Toshiba air-conditioning unit that seemed to be working hard. A steady drip of water fell from it down onto the footpath, where a rivulet had formed, draining the liquid into the gutter.

O'Dea's was just opening up, and a short, dark-haired girl dressed in black with a white apron was placing a new menu into the glass display unit attached to the wall.

"Excuse me. I'm looking for a company called GMC-IT that's located somewhere along here. Do you know it by any chance?" Fahy said to the girl.

"No, sorry. I've never heard of it. But there's some kind of computer place above us here. That pesky air conditioner is always leaking down onto our customers, and the boss has been up to see if they can shut it off a few times," the girl said. Fahy placed the girl as being either from Spain, or perhaps South America judging by her accent and looks.

"Have you seen anyone coming or going over the last few days?"

"No, but I'm not sure I would notice in any case. We are always too busy."

"OK, thanks. May I ask your name?" Fahy said.

"Of course, I am Rebecca, and you?"

"Sally. Thanks, anyway."

Fahy went a little further along the footpath to where a rather shabby red door seemed to be part of the same building, and presumably gave access to the upper floors. But the door was firmly closed, and there were no bells on the door jamb. Fahy knocked a few times as hard as she could on the fading red paint, but there was no response.

She went back to O'Dea's and went inside where preparations for the lunchtime service were in full swing. She found Rebecca again, this time laying out cutlery and glasses on the rather cramped tables.

"Sorry to bother you, Rebecca. I'm actually from the police. I don't suppose there is a back way up to the computer place upstairs, is there?"

Rebecca looked at Fahy in a slightly suspicious manner, even though she had produced her warrant card.

"Yes, I suppose so. There is an iron staircase going up. You'll have to come through the kitchens with me."

Rebecca turned and walked to the back of the dining area with Fahy following closely behind. They entered the kitchens which were frantically busy. Four chefs clad in white were chopping, sieving and frying what smelled like delicious food. Rebecca led Fahy to the rear of the area and opened the back door. Outside, one of the sous-chefs was having a smoke, and when he saw Rebecca, he quickly extinguished his cigarette and went back inside. Rebecca pointed to a rusty brown and rather rickety stairway leading up to a partially glazed door painted in white at the rear of the first floor.

Rebecca went back inside and left Fahy to it. Fahy mounted the old stairs, which had completely rusted through in places, hoping they wouldn't collapse under her. On the landing, she peered in through the dirty glass, but could see nothing much. But she did notice that a very stout black electrical cable was going into the building through a hole that had been cut roughly into the wall beside where she stood.

She tried the door, which had a Yale lock that looked to be quite new. It didn't shift. But when she took out her warrant card and inserted it into the gap between the lock and the door frame, and jiggled it up and down, the lock yielded and the door swung inwards.

Fahy waited for a few seconds, half-expecting an alarm to go off, but none did. She wondered if perhaps a silent message had been sent to some monitoring centre, but there was nothing she could do about that except be ready to advise anyone enquiring that the Gardaí were already in attendance.

She prepared to go in.

Chapter Eleven

The University of Galway occupies a large campus that stretches from the Newcastle Road all the way down to the Corrib River. It is a mixture of different architectural styles. The older buildings were constructed of grey stone that had generally been fashioned into large and somewhat austere edifices, although they were not unpleasant to look at. The centrepiece is a massive quadrangle with an impressive Gothic arch centred between two sets of cloisters, facing out onto a large lawn divided into four equal sections to complete the symmetry of the arrangement. But elsewhere, much newer buildings display contemporary designs in keeping with the times at which they were added.

The IT building was at the very back of the enormous plot. It looked onto the river, and was ultra modern in style, showing a lot of glass and hard angles to the mostly concrete structure, but both staff and students praised the building for its facilities, practicality and relative comfort.

Lyons and Flynn found a space in the designated car park adjacent to the building itself.

"Gosh, this place has spread out since I was here," Lyons said.

"What did you study?" Flynn said.

"Business and Spanish, for heaven's sake. Absolutely none of which has ever helped me to catch a wrongdoer. But it was great fun, and fantastic to be away from home at eighteen. My parents had a farm near Athenry, and it was all work and no play for them. Anyway, let's go."

They mounted the steps at the front of the building and went in through the glass doors. They found themselves in a massive hall with an enormous atrium that reached up to the roof, which, in this part of the building, was fashioned in self-cleaning glass. To one side of the area, a concrete reception desk, manned by a man and a woman, welcomed visitors and saw to the daily needs of the students and lecturers.

Flynn and Lyons approached and spoke to the man, who had a name badge identifying him as Aongus.

"Good day, Aongus. I'm Inspector Lyons from the Gardaí here in Galway. I was wondering if we could have a word with Professor Madden?"

"Oh, hello, Inspector. Hold on till I see if Professor Madden has signed in today. Lectures don't start again till next week, but he could have come in to do some research or something."

The young man busied himself with his PC for a few moments, and then looked back to where Lyons was admiring the impressive interior of the building.

"Professor Madden is probably in his room. If you go on up to his study, you should be able to catch him. It's room IT2-10. Just follow the signs," Aongus said, gesturing towards a very wide and gently sloping concrete staircase to their left.

"Thanks, Aongus."

The two of them went to the stairs and started to climb. When they arrived at the first-floor landing, they followed the well-positioned signage that brought them to Professor Rían Madden's door.

They arrived at the same time as the man they assumed to be the professor was just opening his office. Madden was a tall man, but his stature was somewhat diminished by the fact that he was quite stooped. He had little hair, and what there was seemed somewhat unkempt. But he had a cheerful, ruddy face, and bright sparkling eyes, giving the impression of a person who was totally with it, and enjoying life.

"Excuse me, sir, but we're looking for Professor Madden," Flynn said.

"Well, young man, you have found him. How can I help?"

Lyons and Flynn introduced themselves, showing the professor their warrant cards.

"Excellent. You'd better come in," Madden said. He was clearly enjoying the encounter.

The study was, unlike the professor, neatly ordered. It was a spacious room, with a terrific view from the window out over the river. Madden's desk was a reproduction of something from an earlier era. It had a red leather tooled top, and burr walnut veneer covering all the visible surfaces, but a few knocks here and there exposing the chipboard beneath betrayed its true age. Along one wall of the room there was a sideboard upon which stood an array of vintage laptop PCs from makers such as Amstrad, Toshiba and IBM.

"Please, sit," Madden said.

"What a lovely aspect you have to your office, Professor," Lyons said.

"Yes, indeed. I am the envy of the junior lecturers, but such is the reward for longevity. Not a common attribute in this particular field of science," the man said, somewhat wistfully.

"Yes, I'm sure. We understand that there is some connection between the university and a company here in town called GMC-IT. Is that correct, Professor?" Lyons said.

"Yes, that's right. Gerard McCarthy. A brilliant chap. Did his masters here a few years back. I always knew he was destined for great things. One of my best students ever."

"Yes, well, can I ask what exactly is the nature of the relationship currently?" Lyons said.

"You make it sound quite sinister, Inspector. It's nothing of the sort, I assure you. You see, here at the university we are fortunate to have some very powerful equipment," Madden said, leaning forward as if he was about to impart some closely guarded confidence.

"I can give you the five-penny tour of our computer room if you like. IBM have been generous to us, which is no surprise I suppose, as several of our graduates have gone to work with them. It's what you could call a symbiotic arrangement."

"And how does this involve McCarthy?" Flynn said.

"Well, you see, our mainframe computer has massive capacity, and while we make good use of it all day long, at night it is virtually idle. Or it would be if Gerard wasn't using it."

"I see. Can you explain that a bit more for me, Professor?" Lyons said.

"It's quite simple really. GMC-IT is in the business of data mining. They process literally billions of perfectly ordinary individual transactions, and identify patterns from the data. These patterns are then used by companies all over the world for marketing purposes. It's ingenious, and quite profitable. Gerard pays us handsomely for the use of our systems, and we use those funds to purchase more equipment or software. Another symbiosis," Madden said, leaning back in his chair.

"Do you know what types of information GMC-IT is processing on your systems, Professor?" Lyons said.

"I have no idea. It's part of the deal that we don't pry into it. Gerard said that if anyone got access to his data, it would compromise the commercial viability of his company, so he has a number of storage devices located in our computer suite that only he can get at, and that's fine by me."

"I see. And are you happy that all the data he is mining is completely legitimate?" Flynn said.

"How do you mean?"

"Well, can you be certain that some of that data doesn't belong to some government, for example, and is protected by law? Or maybe some of it could even have been hacked?"

"Good heavens, Inspector, what a suspicious mind you have. Naturally, I couldn't swear to its legitimacy in a court of law, because I haven't examined it. But I'm confident that Gerard acts with probity, so the university has no concerns in that regard. Now, may I ask what exactly the nature of your enquiries is here today?"

"Professor, Gerard McCarthy seems to have disappeared. There was some kind of incident recently out at Kingstown where Mr McCarthy is building a new house, we think perhaps on Christmas Eve. The body of a young man – not McCarthy – was found at the scene, and since then, we have been unable to locate Gerard McCarthy. May I ask when you last had any contact with him?"

"I see. Well, to answer your question, not for some time. The arrangement works automatically, as you would expect. GMC-IT pays us monthly by direct debit, and as long as the equipment is working well, there's no need for any other interaction."

Lyons sensed that the professor was becoming a little defensive.

"May I ask, Professor, how much GMC-IT pays you for the use of the computers?" Lyons said.

"I'm afraid I can't disclose that at this stage, Inspector. It's commercially very sensitive, and it could damage the relationship if the financial details became known generally."

"Very well. We'll leave it at that for now then. But I must ask you if you have any contact of any kind from Gerard McCarthy by phone, email, text or whatever, to contact me immediately."

Lyons gave the man a business card.

"Of course. And likewise, if you manage to locate him, you might let me know – just to put my mind at ease."

"Yes, of course."

Chapter Twelve

Fahy donned protective gloves and overshoes, not knowing what she might find in the rather dilapidated premises. The room she entered was an office of sorts. There was an old, plain brown carpet on the floor, which was wrinkled and creased in various places, and had a number of ugly black stains here and there. The woodchip wallpaper, painted in a bland magnolia colour, was torn down near the skirting board. There was a single fluorescent tube for lighting, suspended by a couple of chains from the ceiling. A very well-used oak desk stood against the far wall, and a tatty brown tweed chair with four casters sat behind it. The wallpaper was marked where the back of the chair had rubbed against it.

There was no sign of life in the place, so Fahy moved cautiously to the interior door of the room, which was painted in white gloss paint with many chips around the edges.

Fahy turned the cheap plastic handle and drew the door slowly inwards. She found herself looking at a landing decorated with the same wallpaper and adorned with more of the dirty brown carpet. As she went out onto the landing, she heard a loud humming noise which seemed to be coming from the room at the other side.

She crossed the landing and turned the handle of the door opposite, pushing it cautiously inwards. She was immediately assaulted by a wave of hot, thick air, and the humming noise became much more pronounced. She entered the room, and was confronted by high towers of computer servers, stacked one on top of another to a height of around two metres. Each computer was black in colour, and had a row of small, coloured LED lights at the front. Some of these were flickering quickly, and Fahy knew enough about computing to determine that this signalled activity of some kind. The servers, some thirty-six in all, occupied two sides of the room, and in between them there was a large Toshiba air conditioning unit, struggling to combat the heat being generated by the machines. A thermometer nailed to the wall declared the temperature to be thirty-five degrees Celsius.

On the one wall that was not lined with computers, there were three grey steel filing cabinets, which were also old, and in poor condition. But the rather flimsy locks that are normally fitted as standard to these things had been replaced by much stouter ones that looked as if they would be difficult to pick.

Tucked in a corner of the room was a table on which stood five flat-screen PC monitors displaying the GMC-IT logo. Each of them had a computer keyboard and mouse attached. Beneath the table there was another pile of smaller black electronic devices. Each one had a row of small green LED lights along its front, and on each, two of the lights blinked rapidly in what appeared to be a random pattern. A multitude of cables ran around the walls of the room, seemingly connecting all this stuff, some of which were brightly coloured red and yellow.

Fahy crossed to the table upon which the monitors were sitting and gently nudged a mouse which was connected to one of the screens. The GMC-IT logo disappeared, and an innocuous plain blue display replaced it with a single small, highlighted panel at its centre requesting a password. Fahy had no clue what the access code might be, so she left the thing alone and turned her attention to the filing cabinets. Making sure that her blue vinyl gloves weren't torn, she approached the cabinet nearest the door and pulled on the top drawer. It didn't budge. She tried all twelve drawers on the three filing cabinets, with the same result.

Fahy went back to the room through which she had entered and went to the desk. She opened its four drawers in turn, but in the first three found nothing other than a few partially expended ballpoint pens, a pair of scissors, a stapler, and a few elastic bands. In the last drawer, there was a single file with several sheets of paper. She lifted the file onto the desktop and opened it. Inside were a series of electricity bills spanning the past two years, and Fahy noted that the amounts were substantial, although each had been paid by direct debit.

Sitting on the edge of the desk, Fahy opened her jacket in an attempt to cool down after the roasting from her visit to the computer room. She called Maureen Lyons on her mobile phone.

"Hi, Inspector. I'm just here in Dominick Street. I found the premises for GMC-IT and I was able to gain access." She went on to tell her boss about what she had found, and asked for instructions.

"OK. We're just on our way back from seeing Professor Madden. Why don't you give John O'Connor a call and get him to come over to where you are and see what he can make of the set-up?" Lyons said.

"Yes, OK. But do you not think we need a warrant, boss?"

"Probably. I'll get Mick to sort that out for us, and I'll make sure it covers your entry to the place too. When John gets there, can you come back to the station? We need to meet up to see where we're at."

"Yes, of course. See you in a while."

When Fahy called John O'Connor, he was delighted to have the opportunity to get to grips with such an extensive IT installation. O'Connor was himself a graduate of University College Galway and had studied under Professor Madden, gaining a first-class honours degree in computer science. O'Connor was a handsome, if rather earnest young man who loved technology. Although he was a uniformed Garda, he spent nearly all of his time indoors, exploring laptops and mobile phones that the detectives discovered during their investigations. At twenty-seven years of age, he was single, and a little bit socially inept. He preferred the company of machines to that of humans, and while he had chalked up some brief encounters with admiring young female Gardaí at the few social events that he had attended, none had lasted more than one or two meetings, and that, it seems, was the way John O'Connor wanted it.

Fahy had instructed O'Connor to enter the premises of GMC-IT in the same way as she herself had. Some twenty minutes after she had finished talking to O'Connor on the phone, she heard footsteps on the old iron stairway.

"Hi, John. Thanks for coming over. I'm not sure what exactly we have here, but there's loads of computer things in the room at the other side of the hallway, and they appear to be up and running. Can you have a look for me?" Fahy said.

"Yes, sure, Sarge. Over here?" he said, nodding towards the door.

"Yes, but you'd better put these on," Fahy said. She handed him a pair of vinyl gloves.

O'Connor put down his own black laptop PC, one he was rarely seen without, to don the protective gear.

"Oh, thanks. I never thought. Are you coming too?"

"No. I have to get back to the station. But I'd like you to figure out what all this stuff is doing, if you can. As we know, McCarthy has a tie-up with the uni, although how that works, I have no idea. And if you can get any clue as to where he is just now, that would be terrific."

"OK, Sarge, I'll see what I can find out. I'll give you a ring if I discover anything worthwhile."

"Great, thanks, John. See you later."

Chapter Thirteen

Back at Mill Street, Lyons brought the team together. She told Fahy about the discussion that they had had with Professor Madden, and Fahy updated them with more information about Gerard McCarthy's office, such as it was, on Dominick Street.

"It doesn't sound as if the professor was best pleased," Fahy said.

"I agree, but I don't think there's anything sinister there. At least, if there is, he covered it well. I'd say he's just bothered that he may lose a revenue stream. For all the appearance of a fusty old don, Madden is sharp enough," Lyons said.

"So, are we any further on with our three objectives, boss?" Flynn asked.

"I'm hoping John O'Connor might be able to find out a few things from the server farm. But failing that, no, we're none the wiser. Any progress on the dead bloke? Do we know who he is yet?" Lyons asked.

Fahy and Flynn looked at each other.

"No. Sorry, boss," Flynn said, looking down at the floor.

"What about this mysterious girl?"

This time Fahy did the honours.

"Not a sign, boss. Sorry."

"Bloody hell. And don't tell me, there's no sign of Gerard McCarthy either, I suppose."

The other two looked down at the floor and wisely said nothing.

"OK. I think we're going to have to get help with this one. We have a dead John Doe, a missing person of interest, no idea about motive. Unless we can unlock this a bit by the end of the day, I'll have to take it upstairs," Lyons said.

She knew what the consequences of that would be. Superintendent Finbarr Plunkett would in all probability look for help from another region, or even Garda Headquarters in the Phoenix Park in Dublin. The case would essentially be taken out of the hands of the Galway team, and their reputation would suffer. She was determined not to let that happen.

* * *

It was a bright winter's day out in the little village of Roundstone. It was cold, but not severely so, and the sun was shining, albeit low in the heavens, making driving a little challenging.

Garda Pascal Brosnan and Garda Mary Fallon, who ran the Garda station at the edge of the village, were sorting out their plans for the day.

"What are you up to today, Pascal?" Fallon said.

"I have to go up towards Recess this morning. Dinny Murtagh wants his shotgun licence renewed, and I'd better inspect his cabinet to make sure it's all secure. They're getting very fussy about these things lately. And while I'm out that way, I think I'll drop in on Tadgh Deasy. We haven't seen him for a while, and Sergeant Mulholland asked us to keep a good eye on him ever since that business with the Northern Ireland registration plates."

"Oh, right, yes, probably a good idea," Fallon said.

"Will you be OK on your own here?" Brosnan said.

"Of course. I'll do a bit of tidying out the back. There are still a few boxes of files that came up from the old station when it closed to be sorted out. I'll be fine."

"Cripes, good luck with that, and watch out for the spiders!"

"Away with ye. It would take more than a few spiders to bother me, Pascal," she said, smiling at her colleague.

"Right, so. I'll be off. Give me a call if anything important crops up."

"OK," she said, but she had no intention of doing so. The two officers were of equal rank, and Mary Fallon was quite capable of handling any incident that was likely to occur.

* * *

Brosnan dealt with the inspection of Dinny Murtagh's gun cabinet without any issue, and drove back towards Roundstone. Tadgh Deasy ran a garage of sorts a few kilometres outside the village. He serviced and repaired cars, tractors and farm machinery, and traded a few vehicles as well from time to time. But without the modern, sophisticated equipment needed to handle today's cars, he was confined to the older, less reliable stock that was still popular in the community in the area.

Brosnan pulled into the yard and stopped the squad car on the greasy surface. He could see Deasy with his head stuck in the engine bay of a rather worn old Peugeot van. Brosnan got out of his vehicle and strolled over to where Deasy was working.

"Morning, Tadgh. How's things?" Brosnan said.

"Ah, ye know, getting by, I suppose," Deasy said extricating himself from the old van.

Brosnan was having a good look around the dirty yard, observing the various vehicles dotted here and there. He looked past Deasy, too, into the darkness of the shed behind the van he was working on.

"How are things with you, Pascal?"

"Ah, busy enough, but nothing mad. But I suppose you heard about that business out at Kingstown?"

"God, I did. There was lots of talk about it in the town. Have you got anyone for it yet?" Deasy said.

"Enquiries are ongoing, Tadgh. I don't suppose you've heard anything?"

"Just a few crazy theories. But when was yer man actually killed?"

"As far as we can tell, it was Christmas Eve."

"God, that's a funny thing then," Deasy said.

"What's that, Tadgh?"

"Well, on Christmas Eve I was here with Shay. We were watching TV, it must have been about half past ten, when a car drives into the yard. I wasn't expecting anyone, but when I went out to see who it was, there was a young woman. Bonny-looking girl, she was, but in a bit of a state. Her car had a shredded tyre, and she asked me if I could do anything for her."

"Did you sort it for her?" Brosnan said.

"I did. She had been driving on the rim a bit, so the whole thing was wrecked. But I had a spare wheel for her kind of car, so I fitted that and sent her on her way. She seemed very upset over a wheel."

"What kind of car was it?"

"A Renault Megane. It was quite old, but was in good shape apart from the wheel."

"Did you get the registration number, by any chance, Tadgh?"

"I probably wrote it on the docket. She asked me for a receipt."

"Have you a copy of the docket?"

"Yes, it'll be in the house in my receipt book. Come on inside. Would you like a cup of tea while we're at it?" Deasy said.

"Thanks, yes, that would be grand. By the way, how much did you charge her?"

"Ah, well, you see, the tyre on the wheel was almost new. And that by itself would have been around €90. So, I let her have the whole thing for €100, including my time getting her wheel off the car, and fitting the new one. She paid me in cash," Deasy said as the two men walked over to Deasy's house and went into the kitchen.

"Sounds like a bargain, Tadgh," Brosnan said, throwing his eyes to heaven.

Deasy said nothing.

Once inside, Deasy put the kettle on for the promised cup of tea, and then went to locate his receipt book.

"Aye, here we are. Renault Megane – supply and fit used front wheel and tyre. And it's dated 24 December."

"And the registration number, Tadgh?"

"Oh, yes, sorry. 08G70816."

"And you're sure that's the right number, Tadgh?"

"Oh, yes. I wrote it down outside when the job was done. That'll be right, don't worry."

"And what about the woman? What did she look like?"

"Tall, well sort of. Shoulder-length hair, and very striking blue eyes. They'd look right through you, if you know what I mean. But I was more interested in her car, to be honest."

"Thanks, Tadgh. That could be helpful. Would you know her again if you saw her?" Brosnan said.

"Oh, God, I'd say I would. Yes, I would, for sure."

"Grand. We'll be off so. Thanks for your help."

Armed with this new information, which Brosnan rightly recognized could be significant, he declined the offer of tea, and left at once to return to the Garda station in Roundstone.

Chapter Fourteen

"Lyons," the inspector said as she lifted the phone on her desk.

"Hello, Maureen, it's Séan here."

"Oh, hello, Séan. What's up?"

"I'm just after finishing a call from Pascal Brosnan, Maureen. He was out Recess way checking out a shotgun licence renewal earlier on for Dinny Murtagh, and he dropped into see Tadgh Deasy on the way back."

Lyons was hoping that Mulholland would get to the point sometime before evening, but she knew the man well enough not to try and hurry him up.

"Oh, right. Everything OK there?" she said.

"Ah, grand. Deasy has been on his best behaviour of late. But he told Pascal that a lassie had come into his place late on Christmas Eve night with a car problem. He said she was right distressed, but Deasy thought that was because her car had been in some kind of incident and she needed a new wheel and tyre."

"Did Deasy get her name, or even a registration number?"

"Yes, well, not her name, but he jotted down the registration. Just a second, now. Ah, here it is. It's 08G70816, and it was a Renault Megane."

Lyons wrote the details on her jotter.

"Did Pascal get a description of the woman from Deasy, Séan?"

"He didn't say, so probably not. I could ask him to go back out and see if Deasy remembers what she looked like if you want?"

"Would you mind if I talked directly to Pascal, Séan?"

"No, of course not. But could you ask him to let me know if there are any developments."

"Yes, of course. And thanks."

"No bother, Maureen. Talk soon."

Lyons put the registration number into the Garda computer system, but it turned out to be bogus. In 2008, Galway plates stopped at just under 9000, so 70816 was a long way out of range.

She called Sally Fahy into her office.

"Hi, Sally. Look, can you put out this registration number? All points – stop-and-detain, person of interest. And could you let the PSNI know too. She may have gone North."

"Yes, sure, boss. What kind of car is it?" Fahy said.

"It's a Renault Megane. I don't have any more information for now."

"Right, boss. I'll do it straight away."

Lyons then called Roundstone Garda station.

"Hello, Mary, it's Maureen Lyons. Is Pascal there please?"

"Yes. Hold on, Inspector," Fallon said.

After a moment Brosnan came on the line.

"Hi, Pascal. Séan tells me you were out with Tadgh Deasy earlier. Did he give you a description of the woman with the car problem on Christmas Eve?"

"Eh, sort of. She had shoulder-length hair, and was possibly in her late twenties or early thirties. He said he'd probably recognize her again if he saw her. I was more interested in the vehicle, and was just glad to get the car's number, so I came back here at once and phoned it through to Sergeant Mulholland."

"OK. Well, I need you to go back out and talk to him again. Ask him for a better description of the woman. Oh, and bring the old wheel off the car back into the station. The registration number she had on the car was a false one. But we might be able to trace something from the wheel. And find out what colour the car was too."

"But the old wheel may not have been the original supplied with the car, Inspector," Brosnan said.

"I know that, but it's all we've got to go on, unless Deasy can come up with something."

"OK. I'll get back out there then."

Brosnan felt his mission was more of a wild goose chase than anything else, but he dared not disobey Lyons' instructions.

"Mary, I have to go back out to Tadgh Deasy's place. Inspector Lyons wants me to bring an old car wheel in. Honest to God! What next?"

"Ah, she'll have her reasons, don't worry. I'll come out with you if you like. I've finished with the boxes," Fallon said.

"OK. Then we could get a bit of late lunch in O'Dowd's after if you're up for it?"

"Great. I'm getting hungry just thinking about it," she said, smiling at her colleague.

* * *

It was a few hours later when John O'Connor returned from Dominick Street. He trotted up the stairs to his desk, his face flushed and his eyes sparkling with energy and not a little excitement. Lyons heard his return, and having given him a few minutes to settle, summoned him into her office.

"Ask Sally to pop in too, John. Thanks."

O'Connor brought his trusty laptop with him, and in a few minutes Fahy and himself were seated in front of Lyons' desk.

"Right. Anything interesting to report, John?"

"Yes, boss, at least I think so," O'Connor said.

"Go on," Lyons said.

"Well, I managed to log onto that bank of servers Sally saw in GMC-IT's offices."

"Cripes! How did you manage that, John?" Lyons said.

"I brought my own laptop and connected it to his network. I have some pretty clever stuff on it, and after about an hour, I cracked the password. After that it was easy."

"So, what did you find?" Fahy said.

"The first, and possibly the most significant, is that Gerard McCarthy still seems to be driving the server farm. He's connected remotely, and is submitting scripts to prepare the data for analysis before sending it over to the university."

"Wow. Did you find out where he is connecting from?" Lyons asked.

"No, that's the problem. He's using a VPN. And he changes the access server every few minutes. One minute he appears in Brazil, the next it's Romania. He's clever. But of course, he could just be down the road. It's impossible to tell."

"So how can we flush him out?" Lyons said.

"I don't know, boss. As long as he's using the VPN, we haven't a hope."

"Hmm… there is a way to do it, boss," Fahy said. She had a conspiratorial glint in her eyes.

"What's that?" Lyons said.

"Turn the whole lot off. Just go back to Dominick Street and unplug the servers, or whatever. Cut off the electrical supply. That should give him something to think about."

"Bloody hell," O'Connor said, "I'd never have thought of that. But you're right. He'd have to do something if that happened. Maybe even come running to the servers. When do you want to do it?"

"We know that he kicks the university systems into life late into the night. Madden said it was after midnight. So why don't we do it at about eleven tonight? That would give him time to get back to Dominick Street to fix whatever problem there was, and still get to use the university computer later on," Lyons said.

"That could work," O'Connor said.

Chapter Fifteen

Pascal Brosnan and Mary Fallon closed up the Roundstone Garda station, leaving the customary notice affixed to the door advising anyone in need of assistance to telephone Clifden.

When they were underway, Brosnan said, "So, Mary, tell me, what kind of Christmas did you have?"

"It was OK. I went back to Kilkenny to my family. My parents are getting on a bit now, but I have a brother and two sisters, so it was good to catch up with them all."

"Where do you come in the pecking order?" Brosnan said.

"I have one younger sister. All the rest are older, and my brother is quite a bit older than the rest of us. But we all get along pretty well. Probably because we don't see each other too much these days. What about you?"

"Ah, it was grand. I stayed close to Roundstone. My brother is married and has a place over near Cornamona. His wife takes in a few guests in the summer, so they are well used to a bit of hospitality."

"What does your brother do?" Fallon asked.

"He does a bit of building and maintenance work, you know, extensions, painting, garage conversions, that sort of thing. Of course, he added the extra bedroom for the visitors onto his own place. You wouldn't believe how much money there is in bed and breakfast. They do very well out of it."

"Did he help you with your own place?" Fallon said.

"He did a bit, all right. But it didn't need much when I bought it. But tell me, Mary, are all your sisters as pretty as you are?"

Fallon was taken aback by his remark, but recovered quickly, although she sensed that her cheeks had gone bright pink.

"Why, Pascal, would you like me to fix you up with one of them?"

Brosnan took his eyes off the road for a moment to look at his colleague.

"Ah, no, you're grand. Sure, haven't I got the best of ye all here with me anyway?" Brosnan smiled broadly.

"We're just here now, anyway. Do you want me to do anything, or can you manage?" Fallon said.

"I'll talk to Deasy. But you get out and have a bit of a snoop around while we're chatting. You never know what you might spot. But try not to let him know what you're up to."

"Righto."

Brosnan pulled the brightly coloured squad car into Deasy's yard and brought it to a halt. The two Gardaí got out of the car, but there was no sign of Tadgh Deasy anywhere.

Fallon strolled off towards the large metal shed that was used as a workshop. There was a single fluorescent tube that barely illuminated the gloom inside, and the floor was slick with oil and dirt. Fallon was glad she was wearing her heavy Garda boots. She took a small LED torch off her belt and turned it on to help her to see what delights might be lurking in the building. As she progressed into the darkness, she observed a pit that had been set into the concrete floor that allowed someone to get to the underside of vehicles without the use of a hydraulic lift. But it, too, was deserted. There was a steel bench against the left-hand wall, and various unidentifiable bits of car engines were scattered around on top of it.

Outside in the yard, Brosnan looked around between the various vehicles stored in an untidy fashion, but could not locate the proprietor. He went to the door of the two-storey house at the edge of the yard and knocked firmly on the well-worn door.

After a minute or two, the door was pulled back, scraping noisily on the concrete step, and Tadgh Deasy appeared.

"Ah, 'tis yourself, Pascal. Twice in two days. To what do I owe the pleasure?"

"Hello, Tadgh. I've been asked to collect the damaged wheel you removed from the Renault on Christmas Eve. I presume you still have it."

Deasy edged out of the house into the yard.

"God, what on earth do you want that for?" Deasy said.

"I dunno. The order has come from Galway. There must be some reason for it, but I'll be damned if I know what. Anyway, have you got it?"

"I suppose so. It must be over there in that pile of old tyres. The fella collects them every two months or so and takes them away for recycling. But he hasn't been here since. Why don't you have a look on the heap and see if you can find it?"

"God, Tadgh, like I would know what I'm looking for. Can you not find it for me and put it in the boot of the squad car?"

Deasy said nothing, but moved away from the door towards the pile of discarded tyres. He stood looking at the collection for a few moments, and then exclaimed, "Here we go. Doesn't it have a Renault badge in the middle of the wheel?" Deasy scrambled unsteadily on the heap and retrieved the damaged item. He carried it over to the back of the Hyundai, and popped the tailgate, placing the wheel into the loading bay. He turned back to Brosnan.

"There you go, Pascal. There'll be no charge on this occasion," he said smirking.

Mary Fallon came back across the yard, and joined the other two.

"Ah, Garda Fallon. I didn't see you there," Deasy said with a rather concerned expression.

"Hello, Tadgh. Have a good Christmas?"

"Ah, ye know." Deasy was still trying to process where Fallon had been and what she might have seen while he was dealing with her colleague.

Brosnan, sensing the tension that had crept into the encounter, broke the silence. "And you're sure that's the right wheel, Tadgh?"

"'tis of course. The very same. But I still don't know what you want it for."

"Oh, and what colour was the car it came off, Tadgh?" Fallon asked.

"Sure, wasn't it pitch dark? I didn't see, nor care about the colour of the jalopy. It was Christmas Eve after all," Deasy said.

"Yeah, but was it pale, like silver, or dark in colour, Tadgh? You must have noticed that, at least," Fallon persisted.

"I told you, I wasn't concerned about the colour of the thing. But I can tell you it wasn't white or silver. Darker than that at least. That's all I can say."

"Righto, thanks, Tadgh. We'll leave you in peace for now. All the best," Brosnan said.

When the two Gardaí had returned to their car and driven out of the yard, Brosnan said, "Did you see anything fishy in the shed?"

"I don't know how on earth he works in that filth. The place is manky. But I didn't see anything that was cause for concern. Not that I'm an expert in car parts!"

"Ah, he's probably being a bit careful just now. He doesn't want any trouble from us. And it's good to drop in on him from time to time to let him know we are keeping an eye," Brosnan said.

It didn't take the two Gardaí long to drive back into Roundstone. Brosnan parked the car at the harbour, looking out across Bertraghboy Bay. The sea was a deep blue and calm, and the view across the bay to the mountains beyond was spectacular.

"God, Pascal, we live in a very beautiful place, don't we?" Fallon said.

"We certainly do. C'mon, let's get some grub. I'm starving!"

Seated in a quiet spot at the back of the lounge in O'Dowd's, Fallon ordered their celebrated seafood chowder with homemade granary bread, while Brosnan opted for a generous measure of smoked salmon salad – another speciality of the house.

While they were waiting for the food to arrive, Fallon said, "What are we supposed to do with that old, busted wheel?"

"I'll give Lyons a call after lunch and see what she wants us to do with it. Would you be OK for a run into Galway later if that's what's required?"

"Yeah, sure. But can I take the squad car? My own is sounding a bit wheezy at the moment. I think it needs a service."

"Should be OK. Leave the keys of your Polo with me in case I need to go out, and you can bring the Garda car back after."

"Cool. I might stay in town for an hour or so, have a quick whizz around the sales. Do you think it would be all right if I changed out of my uniform before setting off?" Fallon said.

"Yeah, of course. If you head in at around four, you'll be off duty by the time you've dropped the thing off anyway, and then your time is your own."

Mary Fallon leaned across and squeezed Brosnan's hand with her own. He gripped her hand in his, and they remained like that, holding hands discreetly, till the waitress arrived with their food.

"Can I get you a drink with that?" the young woman said, placing their food down on the table.

"Just a coffee for me, please," Fallon said. "And what about you, Pascal?"

"Oh, just a sparkling water for me, please," he replied.

The seafood chowder was a meal in itself, and Mary Fallon made short work of it. Brosnan took a little longer to polish off the generous portion of smoked salmon salad, and then the waitress was back to clear away their plates.

"Can I get you anything else, folks?" she said, cheerily.

"No, you're grand. That was delicious, as usual. Just the bill, please," Brosnan said.

Fallon excused herself as if to go to the bathroom, but when she was out of sight of her colleague, she settled the bill at the bar. A minute later she was back at their table.

"Right. Let's go," she said.

"What about the bill?" Brosnan said.

"All done and dusted. My treat," Fallon said, smiling.

"Ah, God, thanks, Mary. I'll get you back another time."

Chapter Sixteen

"Sinéad, it's me, Maureen," Lyons said into the phone.

"Oh, hi, Maureen. How's things?"

"Not great, to be honest. We still have no ID on the bloke we pulled from the hedge out beyond, and we haven't found Gerard McCarthy either, though there is evidence that he's still alive, at least."

"So, what can I do for you?" Loughran said.

"Mary Fallon is bringing in a wrecked wheel off a car that we think was somehow involved in the incident. Do you reckon you might be able to get any information from it that would help us to trace the owner?"

"Wow! I'm not sure. But I'll have a root around when we're finished here, and see what I can find out. But it's a bit of a long shot, Maureen."

"I know, but long shots are all we have at the moment. See what you can do for us, won't you?"

"Yes, of course. When will Mary be here?" Loughran said.

"She should be in around five-ish. I'll ask her to go straight over to you with it."

"OK. Thanks – I think." Loughran laughed a little.

"Chat later."

* * *

"OK, Sally, here's the plan. John is going to go back to Dominick Street at around eleven tonight. He's going to power down all those servers. He says he can do it so that no damage is incurred. We think that might bring Gerard McCarthy out of the woodwork. He will want to see what has happened, and even try to fix the problem so that his workflow isn't interrupted. So, I think we should stake out the offices. Conveniently, there's a restaurant underneath the place. We could blend in there without being noticed, and keep watch in case he arrives. What do you think?" Lyons said.

"It could work, I guess. Who do you want to be involved?" Fahy said.

"It would look more natural if we were in couples having a meal. You and Eamon could pair up, and I might be able to persuade Mick to join us as well. And perhaps we could get John O'Connor and Mary Fallon in on it too, but they'd need to be in plain clothes. Can you have a word with Eamon and John, I'll talk to Mick, and I'll give Mary a call too. We'll need to talk to the restaurant as well."

"Yes, sure. Leave that all with me. I'll see if I can set it up."

* * *

"Hi, Mick, it's me," Lyons said when she got her partner on the phone.

"Hi, love. What's up?"

"I was just wondering if you'd like to get dinner in Dominick Street later on? I fancy O'Dea's for a change."

"Hmm… sounds OK. I've heard reasonably good reports. What's the occasion?" Hays said.

"It's a bit complex, Mick. Some of the others will be there too, but we'll all be at separate tables. And it will be quite late, so have a snack at teatime," Lyons said.

"What on earth are you up to, Maureen?"

"I'll tell you later, but you'll be quite safe. Trust me!"

"Oh yeah?" Hays said, smiling to himself. He knew his partner too well.

* * *

Lyons brought the team together at five o'clock. Sally Fahy had spoken to Mary Fallon, and she was well up for the adventure. She had left the wheel that she had brought in from Roundstone with Sinéad Loughran to explore.

Fahy had no difficulty booking three tables for two in O'Dea's for dinner at half past nine. The hospitality industry was notoriously slack in the period immediately following Christmas, and O'Dea's were delighted to get the booking, even though they realized that it might drag on a little later than they would have liked. Fahy had made no mention of the Gardaí when making the booking to ensure that McCarthy couldn't be tipped off.

"OK, everyone. Here's the plan. We go to O'Dea's between nine-thirty and ten. Mick and I will go in at nine-forty – the rest of you agree times so that we don't all arrive together. Sally, you're with Eamon, and Mary you'll be with John. During the meal, at around quarter past ten, John excuses himself as if going to the bathroom, but instead he skips out the back and up the stairs to unplug the computers. Then we wait. I'll arrange an unmarked car with a plain clothes Garda to park up across the road with a clear view of the entrance to GMC-IT's offices. When McCarthy turns up to see what's gone wrong, we split. Mick and I will go up the back stairs into the place. Sally and Eamon will take the front entrance, and Mary and John can hang around downstairs near the door to O'Dea's on standby in case the wheels come off. Any questions?"

There was silence for a few moments while everyone digested what Lyons had said.

"Do you think some of us should draw weapons, Maureen?" Mick Hays said.

"I don't think so, sir. I doubt if McCarthy will be armed, and there should be enough of us to subdue him without the necessity for guns." Lyons was always careful to respect her partner's higher rank when they were discussing operational matters in the company of other members of the force.

"Very well," Hays said.

"I presume we arrest him on suspicion of murder, boss?" Flynn said.

"Dead right!" Lyons answered.

"OK, so off you go and get ready then. Make sure you have working radios well charged up. Sally, can you organize that for everyone? We need seven in all, including one for the observation vehicle."

"Just one more thing, everyone," Hays said, "have you all got some means of paying for your meal? Obviously, it's a work expense, but we'll need to settle up tonight."

The group all nodded and muttered their confirmation.

When the briefing dispersed, Mary Fallon wandered back with John O'Connor to his desk and sat on the edge of it.

"So, John. You're to be my date for the night?" she said, smiling at him warmly.

"Eh, yeah, looks like it. Are you OK with that, Mary?" O'Connor said, a little apprehensively.

"Yes, of course."

Sally Fahy approached as they were chatting.

"Hi, guys. Mary, you'll obviously have to stay over tonight after the operation. It's not fair to ask you to drive back to Roundstone at that hour. It could be midnight before we've finished up. You can stay at mine. I have a spare bed and I live quite close by the station. Is that OK?" Fahy said, looking from Mary Fallon to John O'Connor in case they had already made other arrangements.

"Yes, thanks, Sarge," she said, "that would be great."

"And we had better be on first name terms from now on, so it's Sally. That goes for you too, John."

"Eh… OK, Sarge," he said, "I mean, Sally."

"So, what time are you two planning to arrive at O'Dea's?" Fahy asked.

"Let's say nine thirty-five," Fallon said.

"OK. Eamon and I will rock up at quarter to ten then. See you later."

"What are we going to do between now and then, John?" Mary Fallon said with a mischievous grin.

"Maybe you'd like to have a quick whizz around the shops for an hour or so. They'll all be open still. We could meet back here at, say, nine o'clock. I have some work to finish up anyway."

"OK. See you later, then."

Chapter Seventeen

Before the rendezvous with John O'Connor, Mary Fallon telephoned Pascal Brosnan to inform him of the revised plans.

"I'll be back as early as I can in the morning, Pascal. Is that OK?"

"Yes, of course. There's no rush. Take your time. I'll open up and keep the place going till you get here. What's this guy John like?" Brosnan said, trying to suppress the slight element of jealousy that he couldn't help feeling.

Mary Fallon recognized the emotion, and was quick to provide reassurance.

"He's a bit of a nerd, to be honest, but nice enough. I'd say he'll be a bit boring. I hope I don't nod off over dinner!"

"Ha, no chance. I'm sure you'll be perfectly charming, and good company. Where will you be staying?" Brosnan said a little nervously.

"Sergeant Fahy has offered me a bed, so I'm all sorted. Listen, I'd better go. See you tomorrow then."

"OK, see you. Mind yourself."

When the call was ended, Mary Fallon wished that it was Pascal Brosnan she was going to dinner with.

* * *

O'Dea's was, as expected, not very busy when the detectives entered in the pre-arranged order. There was one table of four young women who were lively, laughing and joking amongst themselves, and a table of two occupied by a middle-aged couple who were just finishing their meal.

The three couples were shown to tables at various locations around the restaurant that catered for forty-two covers, including six places set up at the bar which sported a variety of wines, spirits and cocktails.

The meal went by without event. The food was excellent, and the service prompt, but not overly intrusive. The serving staff were a bit puzzled as to why their late-night guests were not partaking of any alcohol, but didn't make an issue of it.

At quarter past ten on cue, John O'Connor excused himself, leaving Fallon on her own, and disappeared out through the kitchens. When he entered the kitchens of the restaurant, a chef approached and seemed to be about to remonstrate with the patron who had lost his way while looking for the bathroom. O'Connor silenced the man by holding up his warrant card and putting his index finger vertically up to his lips. "Not a word," he said. He continued out the back door, climbed the rusty iron stairway, and entered GMC-IT's premises.

Intuitively, he didn't like to simply remove the electric power to the servers. Such action could cause data corruption, and it went against the grain with him to do such a thing, but orders were orders. He located the on-off switches at the back of each of the servers, and one by one turned them off. The noise in the server room faded as each of the machines became dormant, until only the drone of the air conditioner remained. When he was happy that all the servers were powered down, he left again, skipping down the stairs quickly, and rejoining Fallon at their table. As he sat down, he nodded imperceptibly to Lyons who was seated at a table nearby.

"How did that go?" Fallon asked.

"No problem. They are all shut down now, and I spoke to the chefs in the kitchen warning them not to say or do anything if McCarthy turned up. I just hope we haven't corrupted too much data."

"Who cares about the data! We're dealing with a potential murderer here, John."

"I guess. I wonder, will he turn up?" O'Connor said.

"Depends where he has been hiding out, I suppose."

The waitress came and removed their main course plates. She returned a minute later with the dessert menu, and Fallon chose sticky toffee pudding with ice cream.

"Cripes! Where do you put it all, Mary? You're so slim," O'Connor said, blushing from his observation.

Fallon just smiled.

Thirty minutes later, just as the diners were beginning to feel that they were overstaying their welcome, a waitress approached the table where Hays and Lyons were dilly-dallying over a coffee. She stood between them, and simply gestured with her finger pointing towards the ceiling. At the exact same moment, Hays' radio burst into life. It was the observation team parked out on the road.

"Suspect has entered the premises through the front door. Awaiting instructions."

As he was standing up, Hays barked into his radio, "Standby."

As previously arranged, Flynn and Fahy, seeing their colleagues bursting into action, scrambled for the front door. Hays went out the back of the restaurant, and pushed his way through the kitchen, quickly followed by Lyons, much to the surprise of the kitchen staff who were clearing up after the evening service. Hays barged the back door of the premises open, and continued on into the yard. He rounded the bottom of the stairs, and started up, using the rather rusty old handrail to assist his ascent. When he was halfway up, and Lyons was two steps behind him, a man came charging out of the office. He crashed down the stairs, knocking Hays backwards as he jumped partly over, and fully past him. Hays fell on top of his partner, and the pair tumbled back down the stairs, landing in a pile of arms and legs on the concrete yard.

"Are you OK, Maureen?" Hays said. He pulled Lyons to her feet, and looked into her eyes.

"Yes, I'm fine. Go! Go! Catch the bugger!" she said.

Hays disengaged and went in pursuit of his quarry. The young man had a good head start, and was right over at the other side of the yard. The absconder leapt at the brick wall, scrambled up, levered himself over the top of the boundary, and dropped into the lane at the far side.

Hays looked at the wall, and grimaced. He knew he couldn't follow, and wisely decided not to try. He got on his radio which fortunately had survived the melee.

"All units, all units. Suspect on the run in the lane to the rear of O'Dea's. Please pursue and head him off if you can. Detain if possible."

Fallon and O'Connor got the message and left the restaurant. Out on the street, they split up, with each going in opposite directions at a brisk trot. Flynn and Fahy had ascended the stairs to the offices, and noted that in the short time that McCarthy had been there, he had managed to restart nearly half of the servers. Flynn took the initiative and switched them all off again. They were just about to leave when Fahy spotted something that McCarthy had left behind in his haste to escape. She took an evidence bag from her pocket, unfolded it, and placed the item inside it, sealing the top carefully.

Gerard McCarthy knew the lanes and backstreets of Galway intimately. He had studied them thoroughly in anticipation of something like what had just happened. The nature of his business was such that he had to be prepared for all eventualities, and his preparedness had served him well recently.

The Gardaí scouted around the area for a further twenty minutes, but it was hopeless. They had been outsmarted by McCarthy, and God knows where he had managed to get to in that amount of time.

Hays called the others on his radio, and told them to stand down. He suggested they should meet back at the restaurant to settle their respective bills, and debrief.

The group of six were despondent when they arrived back. Hays had set the observation car to prowl the streets to see if they could spot McCarthy's truck, but he wasn't very hopeful.

"OK, folks," Hays said, "he's obviously got away. But listen, don't beat yourselves up. I shouldn't have got sandbagged like that on the stairs. That was a bit amateur. And I nearly killed Inspector Lyons to boot."

The team smiled wryly at his comment.

"Let's all away home now," he said. "I'll fix up with the staff here. We can meet in the morning, except for Mary who will need to be getting back to Roundstone."

Fahy spoke up before they all dispersed.

"Just one thing, sir." She held up the evidence bag containing a black laptop PC. "He left something behind. It could be useful."

"Dead right, Sally. Well done for spotting it. Give that to John. John, can you get busy with that thing in the morning and see what it can tell us."

"Yes, of course, sir," O'Connor said.

On the way back to Salthill in their car, Hays said, "Sorry about earlier. Are you hurt?"

"I may have a few bruises that will need to be kissed better later on," Lyons said, "but no permanent damage. What about you?"

"I sprained my wrist. But it's not bad. I'll put an elastic bandage on it when we get home, and it'll be fine in a day or so."

"McCarthy is obviously up to no good. We need to get to the bottom of his operation, and soon."

Chapter Eighteen

The atmosphere the following morning when the detectives gathered just after half past eight was glum. They had all gone home the previous evening with an abiding feeling of failure. Sally Fahy had taken Mary Fallon back to her flat down at the end of Shop Street in the city centre, and the two women had spent an hour or so chatting through the events of the night.

But in the cold light of day, things looked even more challenging for the Gardaí. The only bright spot on the horizon was the seizure of Gerard McCarthy's laptop which John O'Connor had set about cracking as soon as he reached the station. But things were about to change.

"Lyons," she said as she lifted the phone in the open-plan where they were all gathered.

"Hi, Maureen. It's Sinéad. Listen. Remember that old wheel that you had delivered here yesterday?"

"Yes. What about it?"

"Well, as we suspected, there was a serial number on a little label stuck to the inside of the rim. So, I got onto Renault in Dublin, and asked them if it could be traced. They hadn't a clue, but suggested I called Boulogne-

Billancourt, which is where their HQ is located. After a bit of a struggle with the language–"

Lyons interrupted.

"Sinéad, sorry, but I've had a very bad night, and today doesn't look any better. Could you skip to the end for me?"

"Oh, right. I have a proper registration number for the car, and it belongs to a company out on the Mervue Business Park. It's Gregory Millican Interiors and Company, and they deal in very high-end home décor: rugs, wallpaper, expensive ornaments, that sort of thing."

"Thanks, Sinéad. That's fantastic. You should be a detective!"

"It's OK, thanks. I'll stick to my laboratory, although I hear you all had a nice meal out at the taxpayers' expense last night."

"Don't. It was a fiasco. Is the story doing the rounds, Sinéad?"

"I couldn't possibly comment, but yes, of course it is. Never mind. Gotta fly. See ya."

"Hang on. What's the car number?"

"Oh, shit, I nearly forgot. It's 181G6771. OK?"

"Yes, thanks for that. Talk later."

When Lyons had finished the call, she turned back to the team.

"Well, at least we have one good lead now. That was Sinéad. She gave me the details of the car that was seen out at Kingstown the night the man was killed."

"Wow! How sure is she, boss?" Fahy said.

"She managed to trace the details from the wheel that Mary brought in from Deasy. Don't ask me how. Half of it was in French anyway. But I'm sure the information is sound. That's what Sinéad does."

"What do you want us to do, boss?" Flynn asked.

"Why don't you and Sally go out to the Mervue Business Park and see if you can locate the woman who was driving that night. If you find her, bring her in. Don't arrest her. We don't know that she's done anything wrong as yet. Just 'helping with enquiries'. OK?"

"Yes, sure."

"Oh, and go in an unmarked car. We don't want to scare her off. Here take mine."

Lyons handed Eamon Flynn a piece of paper with the name of the firm on it, as well as the keys to her Volvo S60 which was parked downstairs.

* * *

The Mervue Business Park was a section of the Mervue Industrial Estate that had been established by the IDA in the 1960s to bring much needed jobs into Galway. It had been very successful, and had been expanded and refurbished a number of times, so that now it presented as a modern facility with some well-known names in occupation. It had hosted The Galway Technology Centre, PennEngineering, Thermo King and many other established companies, and had been highly successful in attracting well paid jobs into the region.

Gregory Millican Interiors occupied one of the buildings that had been recently overhauled. It had a large glass frontage displaying the exclusive artefacts that they sold, and the premises exuded an air of opulence and luxury.

Flynn and Fahy entered through the electric double glass doors, and stepped onto some expensive solid wood flooring, laid out in a herringbone pattern underfoot. The showroom must have taken up some 150 square metres, and it was obvious that this was no ordinary high street store.

Seated at the far side of the expansive display area there was a receptionist dressed in a soft green business suit. The woman was probably in her late thirties, and was immaculately turned out and spoke with a refined accent.

"How can I help you folks today?" she said, getting up from her perch at the pristine white desk that housed nothing but a huge Apple Mac computer and a very fancy-looking telephone.

"Hello. My name is Detective Inspector Eamon Flynn, and this is my colleague, Detective Sergeant Sally Fahy. Is the manager around?" he said, holding up his warrant card.

"Mr Millican is upstairs with a client. He shouldn't be very long. May I get you a tea, or a coffee, perhaps?"

"No thanks, eh…"

"Sorry, Philippa, Philippa Naughton," the woman said extending her hand which Flynn shook briefly.

Fahy noticed that the woman had a very expensive diamond ring on her wedding finger, and a thin gold wedding band.

"Perhaps you can help us. Can I ask if you recognize this vehicle registration number?" Flynn said, offering Philippa a small Post-it Note with '181G6771' written on it.

"Hold on a sec," Philippa said. She went back behind her desk and fiddled with her computer for a moment.

"Yes, that's Sandra's car. She's one of our outdoor salespeople. Is she all right?"

"Yes, as far as we know. Is she here just now?" Fahy said.

"No, she's out and about calling on businesses. We have an extensive wholesale trade and we supply a number of retail outlets all over the west of Ireland, and even a few in the North. Sandra is one of our reps that cover the territory."

"OK. Well maybe you could let us have Sandra's mobile phone number then?" Fahy said.

"Yes, of course. Just a moment. I hope she's not in any sort of trouble, Sergeant?"

"No, she's fine, as far as we know. We just need to have a word."

Philippa went back to her computer. It seemed like she couldn't do anything without it. She wrote some details down on a page from her jotter and tore it out.

"There you are. She'll be back here later on if you want to call back. She usually gets here at around five o'clock to file her orders and update Mr Millican."

"Thanks, Philippa. What's Sandra's surname?" Flynn said.

"Oh, sorry, yes, it's Ward, Sandra Ward."

"Great, thanks. We'll give Sandra a call and make some arrangement. Thanks for your help," Flynn said.

When they were back outside in their car, Fahy said, "Shall I give her a call?"

"Let's wait till we're back at the station. That way the conversation will be recorded."

Chapter Nineteen

As Flynn and Fahy were climbing the stairs back at Mill Street Garda station, they met Lyons who was on the way out.

"Hi, boss. We got the name of the woman who was driving the Megane out at Kingstown. She is a Sandra Ward. I have her phone number here. I'm about to give her a call," Flynn said.

"Hi, Eamon; Sally. Why do you want to call her? Surely that will just alert her to the fact that we want to talk to her, and she could vanish again. Wouldn't it be better if you tracked her down and brought her in?" Lyons said.

"Oh, OK, yes. We know where she will probably be at around five o'clock. Maybe we could lift her then," Flynn said.

"Yes, much better. Where is she going to be at five?" Lyons said.

"Out at Mervue. She works for a firm out there and she's expected back in at that time," Fahy said.

"Right, well, why don't you do that then? Do you need any help, or can the pair of you manage on your own?"

"We'll be fine, thanks," Flynn said.

"Right. And go easy on her. It would be better if she wasn't all lawyered up when we interview her," Lyons said.

"Yes, you're right. We'll take it handy," Flynn said.

Flynn and Fahy continued on up to the detectives' open-plan office where they found John O'Connor poring over the computer that had been recovered from the GMC-IT offices.

"Hi, John," Flynn said, "any luck with that thing?"

"No, sorry, boss. It's really well protected. There's a BIOS password, and a disk password too. And the trouble is, if I have more than three wrong attempts, the whole thing will devour itself, and we'll never get anything off it."

"So, what are you going to do?" Flynn said.

"I think it will have to go to Dublin. They'll take the disk out and connect it to another system up there and they'll have some sophisticated software that will get them past the password. I'm afraid I don't have access to that stuff here."

"OK. How long will that all take?"

"I'll be able to get it away later on, and they'll have it in the morning. Depending on their workload, they might have something tomorrow. I know a few of the lads up there. I'll ask them to expedite it as it's a murder case."

"Great. Thanks, John. Let me know as soon as you have anything. Oh, by the way, where has Inspector Lyons gone?"

"She didn't say. Sorry."

* * *

Superintendent Finbarr Plunkett had arranged to see Maureen Lyons in the lobby of the Maldron Hotel out by the Sandy Road roundabout. He had ensured that Mick Hays was occupied at a meeting with the local Neighbourhood Watch group, so that he wouldn't happen across them. Lyons drove to the hotel, and as soon as she entered the premises, she could see Plunkett seated over by the window with a tray of tea, two cups, and a plate of biscuits in front of him.

Lyons went to join him.

"Hello, Superintendent. This is all a bit cloak and dagger, sir. What's on your mind?" she said as she sat down opposite him.

"Straight to the point as usual then, Maureen. Can I pour you a cup of tea?"

Lyons sighed a little impatiently, but Plunkett was already filling the spare cup.

"I wanted to have a quiet word out of the station, Maureen. It's a bit delicate."

Lyons added milk, but not sugar, to her tea and took a sip.

"I see. That sounds a little ominous, sir. Have I done something wrong?"

Plunkett sat back and smiled broadly.

"No, no, not at all. Far from it, as it happens. No. You've come to the attention of our senior management in Dublin. It's not surprising. Your name is on the sheet for solving several very nasty crimes here in Galway over the past few years, and the force needs to make the very best possible use of such effective resources."

"And what does that mean, exactly, sir?" Lyons said, but in her heart she had an inkling of what might be to come.

"As you may have heard, or read, the level of violent crime in Limerick is causing us serious concern. It's been suggested that a sort of task force be established to root out the worst offenders and take them off the streets. Such a group would have the power to circumvent some of the more traditional processes in order to get quick results. It would be quite a small, tight group of very experienced officers, and they'd like you to head it up."

Plunkett sat back and waited for Lyons to respond.

"I see. Well, I can't say I'm not flattered, sir. May I ask if this would involve me moving to Limerick to live?"

"This new unit would be billeted in a highly secure location with some very sophisticated measures in place to protect your identity. Specialist vehicles would be provided and, if required, a secondment from the army would be made available to deal with any weapons or explosives that might be encountered. But most of our targets are just thugs who fancy themselves, and of course, there are constantly power struggles amongst them, which often lead to serious injuries or death. Unfortunately, innocent civilians sometimes get caught in the crossfire, so this lot needs dealing with. And soon."

"When is all this due to happen, sir?"

"We are hoping to bring the unit together next month, Maureen."

"I see. Well, of course, I'll need time to think about it, sir. And I'll have to see what Mick has to say about it. How long would the assignment last?"

"We're not sure. Probably six months at a minimum. But maybe longer. And, I'm sorry, but I'd prefer if you didn't discuss our conversation with Superintendent Hays, for now at least. We have to handle this very delicately. Need-to-know only," Plunkett said.

"I don't think that's reasonable, sir. Mick is completely trustworthy, as I'm sure you know. And he is my partner, after all."

"I've been very tolerant of that, eh, arrangement, Maureen. But you must understand that if any whisper of this gets out ahead of time, the entire operation would be compromised and probably doomed to failure."

"I understand, sir. But I think you should leave it to me to handle that aspect of things. As we are on it, who else knows about this?"

"The assistant commissioner and Superintendent Madigan, and possibly one or two senior detectives who will form the rest of the unit with you. That's all, and that's the way I want it kept."

"Very well. Is there anything else, sir?"

"No, that's all, Maureen. Thanks for coming out."

Lyons got up to leave, as did her boss. They walked out of the hotel side by side. At the door, Lyons said, "Just one more thing, sir. What happens if I decline?"

Plunkett looked at her intently for a moment before responding.

"I couldn't possibly comment."

Lyons got back into her car and set off for Mill Street.

She hadn't felt so uncomfortable for some considerable time.

Chapter Twenty

It was starting to get dark when Flynn and Fahy arrived at Mervue to intercept Sandra Ward. They parked at the side of Gregory Millican Interiors' premises, so that they would not be conspicuous, but still had a good view of any approaching vehicles.

A few minutes after they were settled, a two-year-old beige Skoda Octavia pulled in and parked facing the building. A dark-haired woman, probably in her late thirties, and smartly dressed in a green business suit got out. She had a leather document folder in her left hand, and as she walked away from the car towards the entrance to the building she pressed the key fob, and the doors of the Skoda clunked shut. The detectives were pleased to note that they hadn't been observed, at least not obviously so.

It was a few minutes after five when a black Renault Megane drove in and parked beside the Skoda.

"Check the number plate, Sally. I think this is our target," Flynn said.

"Yup, that's our mark. Let's go," Fahy said, opening the door of their car and getting her warrant card out of her pocket. They approached Sandra Ward who had the back passenger door of her car open and was collecting some carpet and wallpaper samples to take inside.

"Ms Ward," Flynn said. "My name is Detective Inspector Flynn, and this is my colleague Detective Sergeant Fahy. We'd like a word please."

Ward stood up, her arms full of the chattels of her trade, and looked around furtively as if to establish if there was any easy escape route, but finding none, refocused back on the Gardaí.

"Yes, but it's not very convenient right now. I have to get these inside and write up my orders. Could you come back tomorrow?" she said, rather hopefully.

Fahy had moved around behind the woman, in case she decided to make a run for it.

"I'm afraid that won't be possible, Ms Ward. We need you to come into Mill Street with us. We have some questions for you."

Ward hadn't given up yet.

"OK. Well, I just need to leave this stuff inside. I'll be back in a minute."

"Put those things back in your car, please, Ms Ward. I'd prefer not to have to arrest you," Flynn said.

Fahy had moved in quite close behind Sandra Ward to occupy the woman's space, and make it clear to her that she had no choice but to comply with Flynn's request. It didn't take Ward long to process the situation.

"All, right. I'll come, but I'm not happy. What's this all about, anyway?"

"We'll discuss it at the station, Ms Ward. Now, please sit into the back of our car with Sergeant Fahy."

* * *

When Flynn and Fahy arrived back in Mill Street with Sandra Ward, Lyons was back as well after her meeting with the superintendent.

Flynn took Ward to introduce her to the desk sergeant, and escort her to an interview room, while Sally Fahy went to find Lyons to bring her up to date.

Lyons was pleased with the news.

"Give me a few minutes, Sally. Then all three of us will have a chat with her. I need to call Mick first about another matter."

"OK, boss. Is everything all right?" Fahy asked, sensing Lyons' unusually sombre mood.

"Ah, yeah, it'll be fine. I'll be with you in a few minutes."

Lyons called Hays' extension, but the call was answered by his administrative assistant, Betty.

"Hi, Betty. Is the superintendent available?"

"Oh, hello, Inspector. No, I'm afraid he's still out with the Neighbourhood Watch people. It must have run on a bit. Can I take a message?"

"No, it's OK thanks, Betty. Just ask him to call me on my mobile when he gets a minute. Thanks."

"Will do. Bye."

* * *

The interview room was chilly, and rather intimidating. The walls were painted in an institutional green colour, and the only window was high up on an outside wall, but contained frosted glass. It was also quite dirty, so the amount of light it admitted was minimal. The floor was covered in grey linoleum, and here and there it was worn through. In the centre of the room there was a steel-framed table, bolted to the floor, and its top was covered in dark green plastic that was originally intended to look like leather, but had given up the subterfuge some time ago. Four orange vinyl chairs were arranged at opposite sides of the table. The only gesture to modernity in the room was a sophisticated recording device that held two cassette tapes, which was sitting on a modern bookcase. The room was lit by a rather subdued single fluorescent tube that occasionally flickered, to add to the discomfort of the occupants.

Lyons and Flynn sat opposite Sandra Ward, and the tape recorder had been pressed into service with Flynn reciting the usual mantra to comply with regulations.

"For now, Ms Ward, you are free to leave at any time. You are simply assisting us with our enquiries. If we need to change that status, you will be advised."

Sandra Ward was a woman in her mid-thirties with dark blonde hair that fell in waves to her shoulders. She had striking blue eyes, and a pretty, but not beautiful face. She stood at roughly five feet seven inches, and was slim, and quite elegant in her navy business suit and fresh white blouse. Flynn could imagine her being quite successful selling high-end interiors to architects, builders and private, well-heeled clients.

"So, why have you brought me here? It's quite inconvenient. Mr Millican expects us to report to him each evening when we have finished work. He'll be wondering where I have got to."

"What can you tell us of your movements on Christmas Eve, Ms Ward?" Lyons asked, intent on getting straight to the point.

"Christmas Eve? Why? What do you want to know about that for?"

"Could you just answer the question, please?" Lyons said. She was looking directly into Ward's eyes, and not blinking.

"Well, as far as I can remember I went out to my parents' house in Derrymoyle on the Headford Road."

"And what time would that have been?" Flynn asked.

"In the afternoon. I had to do some last-minute shopping in the morning, then I drove out after lunch."

"And what about later on?"

"Nothing much. I got back to Galway about six, and then I stayed in."

"I see. That's not really true, is it, Sandra?" Lyons said.

"What do you mean?"

"You were seen much later that evening out near Kingstown. What were you doing there?" Flynn said.

"You must be mistaken, Inspector. I told you, I was at home all evening."

"I don't think so, Ms Ward. Can anyone corroborate your story? Was anyone with you at home all evening?" Lyons said.

"No, of course not. I was alone."

"Ms Ward, do you know a Gerard McCarthy?" Flynn said.

Ward looked away to the far wall of the room, as if trying to recall the name.

"I don't think so. But I meet an awful lot of people in my work, so it is possible. But the name doesn't ring a bell. Who is he anyway?"

"Tell us about your car, Ms Ward," Lyons said.

"What about it?"

"How long have you had it?" Lyons asked.

"About a year. Yes, that's right. I bought it in October, so just over a year."

"And where did you buy it from, Ms Ward?"

"A private ad on DoneDeal, it was. He gave me a good price, because the owner had just been given a company car."

"So, you would have taxed it then, and had it tested by the NCT?"

"Look, what is all this about?" Ward said, looking from one to the other of them in turn.

"Ms Ward, I think it's about time you started being honest with us. Your car was being driven on false plates. Therefore, it cannot have been taxed or NCT'd in the time that you claim to have owned it. Furthermore, we have evidence that places both you, and your car, out near Clifden late on Christmas Eve. So, I'd like you to tell us exactly what you were doing there, and who you were with. Who was the man that accompanied you on your drive out to Kingstown and ended up dead in the ditch?" Lyons said.

"I don't know what you're talking about. I've told you where I was, and that I was alone. Now can I go, please?"

"Absolutely not. Eamon, take Ms Ward out to the sergeant and have her booked in properly. Make sure we get her fingerprints. Arrest her on suspicion of perverting the course of justice, and while you're at it, apply for an extension to twenty-four hours for her detention," Lyons said.

"You can't do that," Ward shouted, "I'll lose my job. This is ridiculous. I want a solicitor, and now!"

"Look after that for me, Eamon, will you?" Lyons said.

"Right, boss," he said. "I'll catch you later."

Chapter Twenty-one

When Lyons got back up to her office, Fahy came in and told her that Superintendent Hays had been looking for her.

"Thanks, Sally. I'll call him now."

"How did you get on with Sandra Ward?" Fahy said.

"I'll tell you later. I need to call Mick."

"OK, sorry, I'll leave you to it then," Fahy said. She left the room, closing the door behind her.

Lyons dialled Hays' number.

"Hi, Mick, it's me," she said.

"Hi. I heard you were looking for me."

"Yes, I am. Have you got a few minutes?"

"I guess. I'm just writing up my report from the meeting, but it could wait, I suppose," Hays said.

"OK. Meet me in the café on the corner in five minutes," Lyons said.

"OK. Is everything all right, love?"

"I'll tell you when I see you."

* * *

Ten minutes later Maureen Lyons and Mick Hays were seated at a table near the back of the café where it was nice and quiet. They had purchased two lattes at the counter, and Hays had offered to buy his partner a cake, but Lyons had declined.

"So, what's up?" Hays said.

Lyons relayed the conversation she had had with Superintendent Finbarr Plunkett.

"Promise me you didn't know about this, Mick?"

Hays shuffled a little uneasily on his chair, and took a sip of his drink.

"I'd heard whispers about the thing in Limerick, but I had no idea they had you down for it, none at all."

"Had you heard who was going to be involved?" Lyons said.

"No. Pat Madigan told me about the new unit, but said it was early days, and they were just getting sorted out before pulling the team together. It's a great vote of confidence in your ability, Maureen, that they have asked you to head it up."

"Do you think I should take it?"

Lyons looked apprehensively at her partner. Although they had been together for some years, they weren't married, and she always had a niggling doubt about their relationship. Not that Hays had ever given her any reason to be concerned. It was just her own insecurity at work, and it surfaced from time to time.

"Tough question. On a personal level, no. I'd hate it. Apart from the separation, I'd be worried sick about your safety. These thugs from Limerick are particularly vicious. They'd think nothing of seeing off a member of the force. In fact, it would be seen as a trophy for some of the scum."

"I guess there's a 'but' coming," she said.

"Not really. Obviously, if you were successful, and I'm certain you would be, it would be a tremendous feather in your cap. God only knows what they would give you next – maybe Assistant Commissioner or something. And here's the 'but' you were looking for."

"Go on."

"I don't think I could handle it, Maureen. I know we have very different careers here in the force, but we can always discuss things with each other when things get tricky, and I rely on you much more than you realize to be effective. And more than that, I depend on you totally at a personal level. I love you very much, and I'm not sure I could manage us being apart. I'm sorry if that puts you in an awkward spot."

Lyons reached across the small table and placed her hand over his.

"Thanks, Mick. I guess that's what I was hoping you'd say, but I wasn't sure. I feel the same, by the way. I don't want to be apart from you. I don't care about the danger. I think I'd be able to handle that. It wouldn't be the first time. But I don't think I could bear to be away from you, even for six months," she said. She squeezed his hand.

They just looked warmly at each other for several moments.

"That leaves us with somewhat of a dilemma for his Plunketness, does it not?" Hays said.

Lyons smiled. "Ah, don't be worrying, love, we'll think of something between the two of us!"

* * *

Lyons got back to the station with a spring in her step. She might be about to flush her career down the drain, but she wasn't worried. Her relationship with Hays was on a sounder footing than it had been, and at that moment she didn't care about anything else.

"Eamon, can you arrange to have Sandra Ward's car brought in from Mervue? Ask Sinéad Loughran to go over it for prints – especially the passenger's side. And ask Sally to pop in for a minute will you, if she's still here. Did you manage to get an extension for us to hold Ward overnight?"

"Yes, that wasn't a problem," Flynn said. "Though the Super did give me an earful about how certain we were that she was involved in the murder. I just trotted out the usual bullshit."

"Good. Well done," Lyons said and went into her office.

A minute later, Sally Fahy appeared in the doorway.

"Hi, boss. You were looking for me."

"Yes, come in, Sally. Grab a seat."

Fahy sat down opposite Lyons, and looked at her boss inquisitively.

"I need you to do something for me. I want you to get onto Roundstone and ask Pascal or Mary to bring Deasy in here for ten o'clock tomorrow morning. I'm hoping he'll be able to identify missy downstairs. Then at least we'll have something to go on. We still don't know who the victim is yet."

"Yeah, I know. It's weird, isn't it?"

"Yes, it is. And if we don't get somewhere soon with this investigation, Plunkett will bring in the heavy mob. And I'm not having that."

Lyons accompanied her sergeant back out into the open-plan area where Eamon Flynn was seated at his desk.

"Did you manage to get a tow for Ward's car, Eamon?"

"Yes, boss. It's on its way. And Sinéad has agreed to stay back a while and give it the once-over before she goes home."

"Great. By the way, Eamon, what did you think of that Professor Madden we met out at the university?"

"OK, I suppose. A bit of a nutty professor. But I did get the impression he was holding something back from us."

"Hmm… so did I. We should have another word with him, I think he has more to say."

Chapter Twenty-two

The truck from Lynch's towing service arrived carrying Ward's car soon after six o'clock. Loughran supervised the operator as he lifted the vehicle using the broad canvas straps and hydraulic equipment attached to the lorry. The Megane swung gently away from the flat-bed and descended onto the tarmac, the canvas straps giving out an ominous creak. But five minutes later, Lynch had detached the gear, stowed it on the tow truck, and disappeared out of the yard in a puff of blue smoke and the grinding of gears.

Loughran and her assistant, dressed in white crime-scene suits, approached the car and started to work on it. Using fine brushes, they applied grey fingerprint powder to the doors, door handles and windows on each side, and repeated the exercise on the rear doors and boot lid. Loughran's assistant easily gained access to the inside of the car using some gizmo that was probably highly illegal, and the two of them went to work on the interior.

"See if there's anything on the inside of the passenger's door handle. That's usually a good place for an errant fingerprint," Loughran said.

After an hour, they had collected a good number of prints on their small clear adhesive sheets, and put them into protective outer sleeves to be analysed in the laboratory.

"Just check the glove box and under the seats, Mark, in case there's anything of interest. I know my car has the ability to completely swallow stuff," Loughran said.

"Right, boss, I'll have a look," the young man said enthusiastically.

Loughran went inside and started to process the various sets of fingerprints that they had collected. It was a painstaking task. Each sample had to be photographed using a specialist camera, and then uploaded to the Gardaí's server that was located in some remote place at the end of a network connection. When she had finished uploading the images, she then set a program in motion that would compare the collected samples to the Garda database of fingerprints that held hundreds of thousands of sets. But such was the power of the computers and software that, if there was a match, it could be found in a couple of hours. Loughran decided to wait for the results.

* * *

Lyons, too, had decided to wait on into the evening to see if anything new emerged from the examination of the vehicle. Their time to hold Ward was limited, and if they were to make best use of it, they would need to act quickly. Otherwise, they would have no choice but to release the woman pending further investigations.

Lyons was almost on the verge of giving up for the night when her phone rang on her desk.

"Lyons," she said.

"Ah, Maureen, you're still there. It's Sinéad. Can I pop over for a few minutes?"

"Only if you can tell me who the victim is and who killed him and why," Lyons said.

"Well, not quite. But you'll be pretty keen to hear what we have discovered."

"OK, then. See you in a few minutes."

Lyons knew her forensic colleague well enough to know that she had something of value. But sometimes she enjoyed prolonging the suspense. A few minutes later she appeared in Lyons' office, smiling broadly. Loughran always seemed to be in a cheerful mood.

"Hi, Sinéad. Come in. What have you got?" Lyons said.

Loughran sat, and put three sheets of paper down on the desk, facing Lyons.

"Well, obviously we found Sandra Ward's prints on the car. But on the passenger's side, we lifted a few that belong to a Jack Lavelle. He was in the system because he was arrested during a student protest out at the university a few years back when he took a swing at one of ours. Apparently, he gave the officer a black eye, but he got away with a caution as the officer didn't want to push it. Lavelle was only nineteen at the time, and Jack Lavelle is our mystery man in the morgue."

"Why wasn't that picked up at the time of the post-mortem?" Lyons said.

"Ah. A bit of a cock-up there, I'm afraid. His prints were taken, and uploaded, but we never searched the database. Too much to do, and not enough people to do it. Sorry," Loughran said.

"Never mind. At least we have an identity now. I presume you checked the prints from the body against this lot?"

"Yes, of course. It's him all right."

"Great. That gives us something to talk to Sandra Ward about, at least. And with Deasy coming in tomorrow to identify her, she'll have some quick thinking to do. Look, can you do me a favour? I have to dash, but could you ask Sally or Eamon to start digging on this Jack Lavelle for me?"

"Yes, sure," Loughran said.

"Right, that's it. I'm off," Lyons said, looking at her watch.

"Hang on, there's something else. It might be nothing, but Ward's car had a spare wheel in the boot, and a jack, all present and correct, but no wheel brace. It looked as if none of it had ever been used, although the spare wheel was flat, so the brace should have been there too, clipped in beside the jack."

"Ah, it probably got lost along the way. I couldn't swear mine is where it should be either," Lyons said.

Lyons got up from her chair and slipped her outdoor jacket on.

"Fancy a quick one?" Loughran asked.

"I'll pass if you don't mind, Sinéad. Mick and I have something to discuss, and I need a clear head."

"Oooh, sounds ominous. Anything I should know about?" Loughran said with a glint in her eye. The whole team had spent a long time wondering if Hays and Lyons were ever going to produce any offspring, and Lyons was getting near the upper age limit for such things.

"Definitely not!" Lyons rebutted.

* * *

Back at home, Hays threw together a chicken salad for Lyons while she went and had a shower. She emerged twenty minutes later with wet hair, dressed in a soft towelling dressing gown.

"Thanks, love. Is there any white wine open?" she said.

"No, but there will be in a minute. Chardonnay OK?"

"Perfect. You really know how to spoil a girl!"

Hays smiled as he went towards the fridge to fulfil her wishes.

As Lyons ate her salad, washed down with a decent measure of crisp white wine, she said, "I suppose we'd better talk about Plunkett's proposal. What do you think?"

"I agree. The first thing we need to decide is if you are interested in the posting. Have you given it any thought?" Hays said.

"I sure have. It hasn't been off my mind since he said it. My answer is that I definitely do not want the gig. But I'm concerned as to how we can get me out of it without causing serious damage to our reputations, especially mine."

"I know what you mean. But I think I may have a way. It's quite high risk, inasmuch as it could backfire badly, and if it does, we would both be in the soup. But it's the only thing I can think of."

"Care to share?" Lyons said.

"Do you mind if I don't? I'd like to keep this to myself until I have given it a go. If it works out, of course I'll be boasting about it forever. If it doesn't – well, I suppose the Aran Islands aren't all that bad!"

"International man of mystery! I get it. But for heaven's sake, don't put yourself on the line, Mick. Are you going to put this masterplan into action soon?"

"Not saying. Now finish your meal. It's getting late," he said, smiling broadly.

Chapter Twenty-three

The following morning, Maureen Lyons was in the station bright and early. She was soon joined by Eamon Flynn and Sally Fahy. She brought them together, and asked John O'Connor to join them too.

"OK, folks, plans for the day. Eamon, you and I will tackle Sandra Ward. Chances are she'll ask for a solicitor first thing. We'll leave it till about ten o'clock when Pascal Brosnan brings in Tadgh Deasy, and we'll arrange to have her bump into him in the corridor, rather than do a formal line-up," Lyons said.

"Will that be admissible, boss?" Fahy said.

"Yes, it will. We'll get Deasy to make a statement afterwards that will tie it up. He can't afford to be uncooperative. It will carry the same weight as a sighting out and about in any case, but I don't think we'll need it. I'm hoping when we confront her with Jack Lavelle's print on the inside of her car, she'll give it up. Though, what it's all about, I still have no idea."

"Sally, I want you to go out to the university with John. Take a photograph of Lavelle with you, looking as dead as possible, and see if you can shake Professor Madden up a bit. I doubt if he's used to dead bodies. But he knows more than he has told us, and I want to know what that is. I have a feeling he may also know the whereabouts of Gerard McCarthy. We just have to locate this guy. And soon."

* * *

Séan Mulholland was just brewing his first pot of tea for the day. He had announced a sort of early spring clean for the station while things were quiet. It had been met with a few grunts from his small squad, but they had to agree that it was overdue, and they settled to the task quite contentedly after their initial, near silent, resistance.

The peace was disturbed by the phone ringing. The Gardaí present let it ring, knowing that Mulholland would have to answer it himself. It was their way of getting revenge for the clean-up task he had set them.

"Clifden Gardaí, Sergeant Mulholland speaking," he said, casting a disparaging glance at his colleagues.

"Oh, Sergeant, it's me, Christine Dalton. I just thought I'd better give you a call."

"Oh, yes, Christine. What can I do for you?" Mulholland's interest was suddenly piqued.

"Well, Sergeant, it's Gerard. I heard from him last night. He just rang to tell me he was OK, and not to worry."

"Did he say where he was calling from, Christine?"

"No, no he didn't. But isn't it terrific that he's all right?"

"Yes, of course, but we need to find him and talk to him, Christine. What phone did he ring you on?"

"How do you mean? Sure, haven't I only the one phone? I don't be bothered with any of those new-fangled mobile things," Dalton said.

"Right. Well, I'm glad he's OK. But if he calls again, Christine, find out where he is and let me know at once. Don't delay, even if it is the middle of the night."

"Are you sure, Sergeant? Once we know he's all right. Isn't that the main thing?"

It was becoming clear that McCarthy's sister didn't really understand the situation, or at least, was pretending not to.

"Yes, of course, Christine, but we still need to speak to him. So, promise me now if he calls again, you'll let me know at once."

"I will, I will, Sergeant. Bye now."

As soon as the call ended, Séan Mulholland rang Mill Street. None of the detectives were available, and he didn't want to leave such crucial information in the form of a message. He tried Maureen Lyons' mobile number, but that went to voicemail, and this time he did leave a message. On his third attempt, he reached Sally Fahy. He told Fahy what had transpired.

"Thanks, Sergeant. I have John O'Connor here with me. I'll get him on it straight away."

O'Connor took the details and phoned a contact that he knew well in Eir, the largest telephone company for Ireland.

"Hi, Brad, I need a favour. I need you to look up inbound traffic from last night for a Mrs Christine Dalton of Shanakeever, County Galway. I imagine it's one of yours, she would have been a Telecom Éireann customer back in the day. She allegedly received a call last night, probably from a mobile. It could have been the only inbound call she received yesterday. I have her phone number here."

O'Connor recited Christine Dalton's phone number that Fahy had taken from Mulholland. He waited for Brad to look it up.

"Here we go. The number that called the Dalton woman was 084 9887642," Brad said. "That's not one of ours. It looks like a burner from one of the foreign companies."

"Any idea where the caller was located, Brad?"

"I can't get that from here. I can put in a request, John, but it will take twenty-four hours or so to come back. And that's if I mark it urgent."

"Could you do this for me, Brad?"

"Yes, OK. If it comes back any quicker, I'll let you know."

"Thanks, Brad. See you."

* * *

Fahy and O'Connor drove into the university campus and wended their way to the back of the site where the IT building was located overlooking the river Corrib. There was a cold breeze blowing down along the watercourse, so the two detectives hurried into the building, which thankfully, was a lot warmer. They asked at reception for Professor Madden, and were, as before, directed to his room further up the building.

Madden was in his study, and looked up to see Fahy and O'Connor coming in.

"Well, well. I do seem to be popular with the Gardaí these days. What can I do for you today?" the professor said, without asking them to be seated.

Fahy wasn't inclined to be intimidated by the man, and asked, "May we sit, Professor?"

"Oh, yes, sorry. Please," he said, gesturing to the chairs in front of his desk.

"As you know, Professor, we are anxious to speak to Gerard McCarthy. May I ask if he has been in touch with you over the last few days?" Fahy said.

"No, no, he hasn't," he said, a little dismissively.

O'Connor spoke up.

"Can you confirm that Mr McCarthy is still using your computer equipment at night to process his data?"

"I have no idea, I'm afraid."

"Well, could you find out for us please? It's important," O'Connor said.

Madden said nothing, but lifted the phone on his desk and dialled. The call was answered a moment later.

"Ursula, can you tell me if GMC-IT are still active on our system at night? Are they still processing in the early hours?"

Madden held on in silence waiting for a response. A few moments later, Ursula was back on, and confirmed that McCarthy's use of the university systems was still going on.

"Thanks, Ursula," Madden said and hung up.

"Yes, he's still using our mainframe at night. Why is that important?" Madden said.

"How is that possible, Professor? I understand that all the PCs that connect to the university mainframe have software on them that ensures only authorized equipment can access it," O'Connor said.

"Hmm… you seem to know a lot about our arrangements, Garda O'Connor."

"I'm right, aren't I? And since we have McCarthy's laptop in our possession, how can he be connecting to submit the scripts to run his programs on your servers?"

Madden said nothing, but it was clear that he was very uncomfortable.

As the silence became a little embarrassing, Fahy cut in.

"Very well, Professor. Thanks for your help. I don't need to remind you that if you have any contact at all from Gerard McCarthy, we need to know about it immediately. We'll leave you in peace, for now."

O'Connor looked a little perplexed, but followed Fahy's lead. The two of them got up and left without further ado.

Outside, when they were back in the car, Fahy asked O'Connor, "What's all that about software for accessing the mainframe, John?"

"It's a security system. It was developed here, but it's used by quite a few state agencies under licence now. It's a good little earner for the college. All of the PCs and laptops that are used on campus, or remotely for that matter, are encoded. They use internet tunnelling to access the mainframe, and a token has to be exchanged between the two machines. If that doesn't happen, or if the token has expired, then access is denied. The cleverness is that each time a handshake is successful, the token is updated, making is virtually impossible for hackers to break into the system."

"So, if I understand what you're saying, and I'm not sure that I do, McCarthy must have access to one of the encoded laptops from the university," Fahy said.

"It looks like that, all right."

"I think we may need to talk to Ursula, don't you? Why don't you go for a walk down by the river for twenty minutes while I see if I can buy her a cup of coffee?" Fahy said.

Chapter Twenty-four

As they had predicted, Sandra Ward had engaged the services of a solicitor. The man, who was not well known to the Gardaí, was in his thirties. He was a tall, somewhat gaunt individual, with a long, narrow face and a small, mean mouth. His head was covered in a shock of dark brown hair, neatly trimmed. His frame was clad in a mid-grey suit which, although fitting him well, did not flatter. As far as Lyons was concerned the final flaw was tan-coloured leather shoes. She never trusted men who wore brown shoes with grey or blue clothing.

Lyons and Flynn entered the interview room where the solicitor and the young woman had been in conference for a full half hour.

"Good morning," Lyons said. She introduced herself and her colleague.

"Martin Gilhooly," the grey-suited solicitor said, extending his hand to be shaken, "I'm here to represent Ms Ward's interests." He made a very obvious gesture by looking at his expensive wristwatch and said, "Can we get on? I have other appointments this morning."

Lyons responded to the cue.

"If you'd rather leave us to it, Mr Gilhooly, please don't let us detain you."

Gilhooly sat down with a rather sour expression, opened his leather briefcase, and withdrew a yellow legal pad and an expensive Montblanc pen.

Flynn switched on the recorder in the room and recited the necessary introduction.

"Ms Ward," Lyons said, "I'm sure you are aware that it is an offence under the Road Traffic Act to use a vehicle on the public road with false number plates, no tax, and no valid insurance."

"It is insured," Ward responded.

"Inspector," Gilhooly interjected, "I thought we were here to discuss the disappearance of Gerard McCarthy."

"No, Mr Gilhooly. We are here to discuss the murder of Jack Lavelle."

Ward flinched, and Gilhooly looked at his client in surprise, although he recovered quickly.

"Inspector, my client knows nothing of the matter you have raised. I was led to believe that we were here to talk about Gerard McCarthy," Gilhooly said.

"I'm afraid you have been misdirected, Mr Gilhooly. While we are indeed anxious to speak to Mr McCarthy, and as of now, we do not know where he is, that's a secondary matter. Now, Ms Ward, how do you know Jack Lavelle?"

"I don't. I've never met the man. Who is he?"

Gilhooly was looking a little concerned at his client's statement.

"That's interesting. We have a witness that says you were seen in the company of Mr Lavelle at Kingstown on the night of Christmas Eve last. How do you explain that?"

Ward looked plaintively at her solicitor.

"My client has told you, Inspector, she doesn't know this Lavelle. Who is he, and why the interest?"

"Mr Lavelle was killed at Kingstown on Christmas Eve. Your client may well have been the last person to see him alive. So, this is a murder enquiry that your client is somehow involved in. It would be wise for her to be truthful with us. Tell me, Ms Ward, did your vehicle suffer a flat tyre on the night of Christmas Eve near Roundstone?"

"No, of course not. I wasn't there. I was at home in the city that night."

Flynn chose his moment carefully to intervene.

"Ms Ward, may I have your mobile phone please?" he said.

"Why?" she snapped.

"Just give it to me please," Flynn said.

Ward looked at Gilhooly who nodded imperceptibly. She reached into her jacket pocket and produced her phone.

Eamon Flynn took the phone, excused himself and left the room.

"So, is there anyone who can corroborate the fact that you were at home on Christmas Eve, Ms Ward?" Lyons said.

"No. I was on my own."

"I see. Tell me, Ms Ward, how do you know Gerard McCarthy?"

Again, Ward looked to her solicitor for confirmation to divulge their carefully prepared response.

"I've been out with him a few times. Nothing serious. Just a casual thing, really."

"And when did you last see him?" Lyons said.

"I think it was Halloween. Yes, that's right. We went to a party together."

"Have you seen him since?"

"We've had a drink once or twice, but that's about it."

"When was the last time you went for a drink with him?" Lyons said.

"I really can't remember. A few weeks ago, I suppose."

"Do you know where he is now?"

"No, of course not. Why would I?"

"How did you meet Mr McCarthy, Ms Ward?"

"We were in college together. But we didn't know each other then. I met him after we had left, and we sort of hit it off."

Just then, Eamon Flynn re-entered the room.

"Sorry to be a nuisance, folks, but we need to move to another room," Flynn said.

"Really, Inspector. This is all very tiresome. And as I've said, I'm under pressure for time," Gilhooly said.

"Mr Gilhooly, if you have somewhere else to be, then I suggest you leave straight away. We will, of course, be continuing to question your client, as we are fully entitled to do. It's up to you," Lyons said.

Gilhooly sighed heavily, mostly for effect, but said nothing in reply.

The four of them shuffled awkwardly out through the door of the interview room into the corridor, led by Lyons. On cue, Pascal Brosnan and Tadgh Deasy appeared at the other end of the narrow passageway and side-stepped right past them. Deasy took a good look at Sandra Ward. Flynn hung back to speak to Tadgh Deasy, and received his verbal confirmation that Sandra Ward was indeed the woman who had called to his premises with a damaged wheel on Christmas Eve.

When Flynn, Lyons, Gilhooly and Ward were seated in the other room, Lyons re-opened the discussion.

She started by removing a piece of paper with a scan of a fingerprint from her folder.

"I'm showing Ms Ward exhibit C-9. Ms Ward, this is a copy of a fingerprint we lifted from the inside of the passenger's door handle of your car earlier today. The fingerprint matches that of Jack Lavelle. Obviously, he's been in your vehicle at some stage."

Gilhooly extended his arm and placed a hand on his client.

"Inspector, as you are well aware, that means nothing. That could have happened at any time, and does nothing to indicate that my client knew this Lavelle person."

"I disagree. It demonstrates clearly that Lavelle has been a passenger in your client's car. A fact which has been substantiated by a witness," Lyons said.

"But that could have happened at any time in the past, probably before my client acquired the vehicle," Gilhooly said smugly.

"I think, Mr Gilhooly, that is a bit of a stretch, even for you, do you not think?"

Gilhooly said nothing.

Flynn, who had come back into the interview room, spoke up.

"Ms Ward, we now have further information about your movements on Christmas Eve. The owner of the garage that you called to when your tyre was shredded has identified you, and is making a statement to that effect as we speak. So, I think you have some explaining to do."

Gilhooly threw his head back, and said, "Cheap trick, Inspector. Very cheap."

"Mr Gilhooly, I don't think you quite appreciate the seriousness of your client's situation. Firstly, she has lied to us concerning matters pertinent to a murder enquiry. Furthermore, she was seen in the company of the deceased shortly before he was brutally murdered. Now, we're going to leave you for twenty minutes to confer with your client. But when we return, I want some straight answers. Otherwise, I'll be charging Ms Ward with obstruction – at least," Lyons said.

When Lyons returned to the room, it was clear that Gilhooly had been earning his keep.

"My client would like to, eh, clarify a few matters for you, Inspector."

"I see. Go ahead, Ms Ward," Lyons said.

"I did drive Jack Lavelle out to Kingstown on Christmas Eve," Ward said. "He said he was going to see

Gerard McCarthy. They had some business to conclude. So, I dropped him at the building site. I waited a few minutes, and it was clear he was settling in for a bit of a session, and I left them to it. I set off back to Galway, but along the way, my car ran off the road a bit and I damaged a wheel. You know the rest."

"How did you know Jack Lavelle?" Lyons asked.

"He was in college with Gerard and me. We used to hang out together."

"And are you saying that the last time you saw Lavelle, he was in rude health in the company of Gerard McCarthy?"

"Yes. That's exactly what I'm saying."

At this point, Gilhooly butted in.

"I think my client has answered all your questions, Inspector, so if you don't mind, we'll be on our way."

Lyons remained silent for a few minutes.

"Very well. But we may have more questions for Ms Ward, so don't go too far."

Chapter Twenty-five

Fahy found Ursula Kenny in the computer suite of the university, which was, thankfully, well away from Professor Madden's study. The suite had a full-length glass wall onto the corridor, and immediately inside that, there was an office arranged in a typical layout with two desks, some filing cabinets, and a bookcase laden with technical manuals.

Fahy could see a woman inside whom she assumed was Kenny. She knocked on the door, and the woman got up from her desk and opened it.

"Sorry to disturb you, but are you Ursula, by any chance?" Fahy asked.

"Yes, that's right. Who wants to know?"

Ursula Kenny was in her twenties. She had long, dark brown hair which fell on both sides of her rather round face. She was probably five feet four inches tall, and a little on the heavy side. She was dressed in a loose-fitting cotton top and blue jeans with newish-looking trainers on her feet.

"My name is Detective Sergeant Sally Fahy. I'm with the Galway police. Would it be OK if we had a word?"

Kenny looked back into the room rather nervously, as if to confirm that there was no one else present, and said, somewhat hesitantly, "Yes, I suppose. Come in."

Fahy followed Kenny into the room, and took a seat alongside her in the spare chair.

"What's on your mind?" Kenny said.

"I'm not sure if you have heard, but we are trying to locate a Mr Gerard McCarthy. I understand he has some connection to the college here," Fahy said.

Kenny looked down to the floor and shuffled uneasily in her seat. After a moment, she looked back at Fahy.

"What makes you think I can help you with that?"

Fahy sensed the woman's unease.

"Look, would it be easier if we went for a coffee or something, or maybe talked outside in the grounds?"

"Yeah, OK. I could do with a coffee," Kenny said.

The two women made their way along the corridors to the cafeteria that was positioned near the entrance to the IT building. Fahy ordered coffees for them both, and then she said, "Let's go outside."

They walked out into the cool winter sunshine, and strolled along the grass that lay between the building and the river.

"So, Ursula, what can you tell me about Gerard McCarthy?"

"I do know Gerry. He's really nice. He has some arrangement with Professor Madden to use our mainframe overnight. He runs a data mining company, as far as I understand it. I'm not familiar with the actual programs he runs, but I do some file transfers for him sometimes, and his stuff is included in our nightly backups," Kenny said.

"When did you last see him?"

Kenny looked away and said, "It was before Christmas. I can't remember exactly when."

"So, you haven't seen him since Christmas at all, then. Are you sure, Ursula?"

"I told you. Why? Is he in some kind of trouble?"

"Have you ever heard of a man called Jack Lavelle, Ursula?"

"No, I don't think so. Why?"

"What can you tell me about the special software that only allows specific PCs to access the college mainframe?" Fahy said.

"Oh, yes, that's right. When we get a new batch of laptops in from Dell, or Lenovo, I have to put that software on them before they are issued to staff or students. It doesn't take long, but it's important."

"And who controls the university's inventory of laptops, Ursula?"

"I do. We supply machines to some of the grant-aided students who can't afford their own, and of course we give the college staff laptops too. If a student has their own one, we have to put the software on it before they can use it. But they don't object, because they get an educational copy of Office 365 for free as well, and some other stuff like anti-virus software and a secure web browser."

"Ursula, we know that Gerard McCarthy has very recently acquired a replacement laptop. We have the one he was using back at the station. He's been logging on to your mainframe in the evenings to submit his jobs, and he can't do that unless he has an encoded machine. Did you give it to him?"

Kenny said nothing for a good few moments. Fahy was happy to let her figure out her next move.

"I suppose I may as well tell you. Gerard did contact me. It was our first day back after Christmas. He said he needed a new encoded laptop, but he didn't want anyone to know about it. I took a new Lenovo from the store and gave it to him. Am I in trouble?"

"Ursula, I don't care one little bit about your stock of computers. That's between you and the college. But I need to know about where you met McCarthy, and when."

"I have a flat in town. He came to my place and I handed it over. Perhaps I should explain. We had been seeing each other."

"I see. Do you know where he is now?"

"No, I swear. He said he might have to go away for a bit. He didn't seem himself."

"Do you have a mobile number for him, Ursula? It would be best if you tell the truth now. This is a serious business," Fahy said.

Kenny said nothing for another few moments.

"It's on my phone back in the office," Kenny said.

They had almost circumnavigated the building by now, so it didn't take them long to get back to the computer suite. Kenny retrieved her phone from her desk drawer, scrolled through the list of contacts, and scribbled a number down on a piece of paper. She handed it to Fahy.

"Thanks, Ursula. Now, if Gerard contacts you, please don't tell him about this conversation. Leave it to us, please. And don't call him either. If you do try to make contact with him, it could land you in serious difficulty. Trust me."

Fahy left the building and found John O'Connor sitting on a bench overlooking the river Corrib.

"Hi, John. Nice here, isn't it?" she said.

"A bit cool, but pleasant enough. Did you find Ursula?"

Fahy waved the piece of paper with Gerard McCarthy's phone number on it in the air.

"I did. And I got Gerard McCarthy's proper mobile number too! Let's get back and tell the boss."

"Wow! Well done you. We might even be able to locate him now that we have that."

Chapter Twenty-six

Superintendent Mick Hays knocked on his boss's door with some trepidation. He needed Plunkett to be in a good humour for what he had in mind, and he knew well that such a thing could not always be guaranteed.

A loud invitation came from inside the office, and Hays went in.

"Ah, Mick, 'tis yourself. Come in. Take a seat. What can I do for you?"

"Good morning, sir. I was hoping to have a word with you about this thing in Limerick you have been speaking to Inspector Lyons about."

Plunkett was clearly a little surprised at the topic being raised by Lyons' partner.

"Oh. Right. But would it not be better if the inspector came directly to me to discuss it, Mick?" Plunkett said.

"Maureen has asked me to have a chat with you about it, sir, off the record, as it were," Hays said. He was well used to reading Plunkett's frame of mind, and so far, he wasn't alarmed at the reaction he had received.

"Very well. What's the story?"

"Maureen is obviously very flattered to have been asked to take charge of such a high-profile unit, sir. She really appreciates the recognition she has been shown, and furthermore, I believe she would do a fine job with what is proposed," Hays said.

"Yes, Mick, all very good, but I sense there is a 'but' coming."

"That's just it, sir. We've talked it over quite thoroughly, and Maureen is minded to decline the offer. But she is very concerned that it could affect her career in a negative way, and of course, she doesn't want to look a gift horse in the mouth, either."

"Hmm… I see what you mean. May I ask why she doesn't want to take this somewhat unique opportunity?" Plunkett said.

"It's complicated, sir."

"Isn't it always where women are involved, Mick?" Plunkett said. He had a wry smile on his face.

"Just between us, sir, it's more to do with our relationship that anything else. She's not scared of working to take down some of the toughest criminals in the country. I think you know her well enough to know that she has no fear of villains. But she's concerned that it could mean the end of the road for the two of us. And neither of us wants that," Hays said.

"I see. Well, as you know, Mick, I've had some misgivings about the nature of your relationship ever since Inspector Lyons moved in with you. And now it looks as if I had just cause," Plunkett said.

The two men remained silent for several minutes.

"So, just to be clear, you are saying that Inspector Lyons is not going to take up the offer then?" Plunkett said.

"Yes, sir, that's about the size of it. But I'm afraid there's more."

Plunkett now looked a little alarmed.

"We were hoping you could square it off with HQ, sir. I know it's a lot to ask, but we think it's the only way to protect her position. If you could somehow scupper the idea up above, then she might just get out of it unscathed," Hays said.

"Jesus, Mick. You're asking a lot. Doing that could bring my judgement into question, too, and I can't be having that."

"Will you at least think about it, sir?"

More silence.

"Ah, to hell with it," Plunkett said, slapping the palms of his hands down noisily on the top of his desk, "sure, I'm nearing retirement anyway. What can they do to me at this stage? Right. I'll stick my arse out the window for you both, and hope for the best. I'll make up some bullshit like we can't do without Inspector Lyons here for lots of reasons, and tell them they'll have to find someone else. But I'm telling you, Mick, if I ever need you to do anything for me in return, I'll expect your cooperation."

"That goes without saying, sir, of course. And thanks, it means a lot to us both," Hays said.

"I know it does, and that's why I'm doing it for you. This job isn't kind to relationships, Mick, as I know only too well. My own marriage fell apart when I was just a DI some years back, and there's no doubt in my mind, it was the job that did it. Mary spent days and nights at home worrying if I'd come home injured or beaten up, or worse still, in a wooden box. Those were tough times hereabouts. After a while she couldn't take it anymore and she left me. And I can't say I blame her. You have a good thing going with Lyons, I can see that, and believe me, it's worth fighting for. Though why you won't make an honest woman out of her is beyond me."

Hays smiled.

"That's another day's work, sir. But thank you. Sincerely. I mean it," Hays said.

"Is there anything else, Mick, although I'm nearly afraid to ask?"

"No, sir, nothing else."

"Right. Well, you'd better leave me to destroy my career all by myself then, hadn't you?" Plunkett said.

"I hope it doesn't come to that, sir."

"Ah, away with you. It'll be fine."

Hays knew that Plunkett was astute enough to wiggle his way out of the dilemma that he had been placed in. But he was grateful to the senior man, who had shown a little more compassion than Hays would have given him credit for.

Chapter Twenty-seven

When Fahy and O'Connor got back to the station, O'Connor went off to delve into the phone number that Ursula Kenny had given them, while Fahy went in search of Lyons to bring her up to date. She found Lyons in her office.

"Hello, boss. Got a minute?" Fahy said.

"Sure, Sally, come in, grab a seat," Lyons said, pushing the keyboard of her PC away to the side.

"Any news?" Lyons said.

Fahy brought Lyons up to date with the information they had gleaned from the university.

"Excellent. I hope it doesn't take John long to discover where McCarthy's phone is located. I presume that's what he's doing?" Lyons said.

"Yes, I presume so. Anything new here?"

Lyons remained pensive for a minute, then she said, "Close the door, Sally."

Fahy did as she was asked and sat back down in front of her boss.

"I shouldn't really be telling you this, so Scout's honour, not a word to anyone, OK?"

"Yes, OK."

Lyons told Fahy about the position in Limerick that she had been invited to apply for.

"Wow! Congratulations to you, boss. I guess you're going to take it?" Fahy said.

"It's not quite as simple as that, Sally. I've talked it through with Mick a few times – in fact we've hardly talked about anything else since I was offered the job. But neither of us wants to be separated from each other, especially in a situation where I would be involved in all sorts of God knows what. I don't think the relationship could take it, and neither of us want to run the risk. What do you think?"

Like every good Libran, Fahy could see both sides of the argument, and responded accordingly.

"Well, it's a terrific opportunity. I mean, if it went well, you'd almost certainly be made up to Detective Superintendent, and that would be amazing. But on the other hand, I can see that it could put a lot of strain on your relationship. Could Mick… eh I mean Superintendent Hays, get a posting to Limerick too, perhaps?"

"No. That's out of the question. His future lies here. When Plunkett retires in a couple of years, Mick will be a shoo-in for that role, and it would be selfish of me to upset his applecart. Anyway, there might not be a vacancy in Limerick that would be suitable for him."

"So, what are you going to do?" Fahy asked.

"Mick says he has a plan, but he wouldn't tell me what it is. If it works though, you'll be stuck with me for a while yet. I'm only telling you, cos it could have an impact on your career progression too."

"How's that?" Fahy said.

"Well, if I moved on, you'd surely be in line for DI, but if I don't, you'll be stuck with DS for God knows how long, and that's hardly fair, is it?"

"Look. Don't you worry about me. If I want inspector that badly, and by the way I don't, not yet anyway, I can always move to another station or another area. But for now, at least, I'm perfectly happy as a detective sergeant, especially working with yourself and Eamon. And to be honest, Maureen, I'd be more than a little pissed off if you left us."

Lyons stood up, came around the desk, and gave Fahy a quick hug.

"Thanks, Sally. That means a lot to me. Right! Why don't you go and see what our favourite techy nerd is up to? I have some emails to see to."

"Sure. But do let me know how Mick gets on with the Super, won't you?"

"Yes, of course."

* * *

Fahy went back outside and walked over to where John O'Connor was, as usual, running two PCs simultaneously.

"Hi, John. Did you get anything from that phone number we got from Ursula Kenny?"

"Hi, Sarge. I'm just waiting for the airtime provider to come back to me with the details. But there is something a bit odd," O'Connor said.

"Go on."

"Well, the phone is actually turned on at the moment. And you'll never guess where the signal is coming from."

"You're right, John, I'll never guess. For fuck's sake just tell me!"

"Sorry, Sarge. It's only coming from the mast attached to Clifden Garda station. That mast is pretty tall. It covers quite a big area. I can't get another ping from another mast to pinpoint it yet, but it's definitely somewhere near the cop shop out there."

"Bloody hell! I'd better tell the boss. You are sure, aren't you?"

"Yes, no doubt about it. But there's something else too."

"Jesus, John. This is like separate episodes of *Morse*, a week apart. Tell me for fuck's sake!"

"Sorry, Sarge. He's using his phone as a Wi-Fi hotspot to move data."

"What does that mean?"

"It means he probably hasn't got broadband wherever he is. Otherwise, he'd be using that. It's much quicker."

"Hmm… interesting. OK, thanks."

Fahy went back to tell Lyons what John O'Connor had discovered.

"Blimey," Lyons said, "talk about cheeky. I'd better give Séan a call and let him know. Are you OK to dash out there with me if necessary, Sally?"

"Yes, of course. Shall I hold on?"

"Tell you what. Why don't you grab us a couple of coffees, and I'll call Clifden while you're gone?"

"Right. I'll be back as quick as I can."

When Fahy had left the office, Lyons called Séan Mulholland.

"Hi, Séan, it's Maureen."

She went on to tell Mulholland what had been discovered about Gerard McCarthy's phone. Mulholland was clearly not amused.

"Do you want me to come out there, Séan? I can be there in an hour or so and we could see what's going on then," Lyons said.

"No, no thanks, Maureen. This is something I'll have to do for myself. I'll not have the likes of him taking liberties on my patch. Leave it with me. I'll be in touch." Mulholland hung up the phone before Lyons could respond.

Mulholland was furious. He felt that McCarthy was making fools of the lot of them, and although he was generally quite relaxed in carrying out his work, he was not one to be messed about. McCarthy would rue the day he tangled with Sergeant Séan Mulholland.

Mulholland went to the safe that was cemented into the back wall of the station and opened it with the key that he kept constantly in his uniform pocket. He reached in and found the gun that he had there for serious incidents which, thankfully, were rare in this part of the country. He counted out ten bullets, and took a spare magazine with another ten in it as well.

"Jim!" Mulholland shouted across the room.

Jim Dolan got up from his desk and walked across to where Mulholland had the weapon laid out on a spare desk.

"I need you to countersign this for me. I have the gun and twenty live rounds. Let's hope we'll not be needing them."

Dolan looked solemnly at his boss. Neither of them liked firearms of any kind, but occasionally they needed to equip themselves for unforeseen eventualities, and at those times, Mulholland's firearms training came in very handy.

Jim Dolan counted the bullets that Mulholland had set out on the table, and countersigned the documentation. Mulholland made sure that the safety catch on the gun was on, and slipped the weapon onto the side pocket of his uniform jacket.

"Thanks, Jim. Now get Peadar and make sure you both have working radios. We're going for a drive. Three separate cars, OK?"

Jim Dolan recognized that his boss was in no mood for explanations.

"Yes, right away, boss. Where are we off to?"

"You'll see. I'm in the lead car. You just follow till I tell you to stop."

Chapter Twenty-eight

The convoy of Mulholland's Saab, Jim Dolan's blue Ford Mondeo and Peadar Tobin's brightly coloured Hyundai squad car set off from the Garda station, taking the N59 Westport Road out of the town.

When they got to the sharp bend in the road where the turn to the right for Shanakeever was signposted, Mulholland put on his indicator and turned in. He slowed to a gentle pace, and drove along the narrow single-track lane till it forked just after Clifden Garden Services, with the right-hand leg going on down to Shanakeever Lough itself, and Christine Dalton's bungalow.

Mulholland stopped the car in the road, and got out. He walked back to the brightly coloured squad car, and as he approached, Peadar Tobin lowered the driver's window.

"You stay here, Peadar. Park this thing across the road, and don't let any bugger past you whatever the circumstances. If you see anything – anything at all – call it in on the radio. Got it?"

"Yes, Sarge. No problem."

Mulholland then walked to the driver's side of Jim Dolan's car, where the window had already been opened.

"Jim. Stay close to me. I'll be pulling up a wee bit short of the house. Then I want you to go around the back. Keep out of sight. There's a dry-stone wall you can go behind. I want the rear of the house covered in case chummy makes a break for it. And see if there's any kind of vehicle anywhere about too. OK?"

Back in his car, Mulholland set off again towards Shanakeever Lough. About 150 metres before Christine Dalton's house, he pulled the car up onto the grassy verge and turned off the engine. He got out, and signalled Dolan to go around the back. Mulholland walked in silence to the front of the little cottage, and thumped three times with the side of his fist on the door.

After a few moment, Christine Dalton opened it, and looked at Mulholland with surprise.

"God, it's yourself, Sergeant. Have you news?" she said, wringing her hands.

Mulholland just stared coldly at the woman with his arms folded in front of his chest for what seemed like an age. When the silence was starting to become embarrassing, he said, "I thought better of you, Christine. Are you going to bring him out, or are we coming in?"

"I don't know what you mean, Séan. What are you on about?" Dalton said.

Mulholland detected movement at the back of the property, and looking beyond Christine Dalton, he could see a man hurrying towards the back door with a laptop under his arm and a backpack in his other hand.

"Stand aside, Christine," Mulholland said. At the same time, he pressed the transmit button on his radio which was pinned to his lapel. "He's coming your way, Jim. Don't let him get away."

Jim Dolan had positioned himself next to an old ramshackle shed, with a rusty tin roof and crumbling walls, inside which there was a dirty Toyota Hilux parked.

McCarthy scrambled across the uneven ground, heading for the shed, but as he approached, Dolan held up the set of keys that he had removed from the ignition of the Toyota, and said calmly, "Are you looking for these?"

McCarthy turned and ran towards the road, but Mulholland, anticipating the move, had positioned himself to cut off the fleeing suspect. He withdrew the gun from the side pocket of his jacket, pointed it at the running fugitive and said, "Enough. Stay where you are, hands where I can see them."

Mulholland called Peadar Tobin on the radio, and told him to come on up to the house in the squad car.

When he arrived after a couple of minutes, he joined Mulholland, Dolan and their quarry. McCarthy had had the good sense not to tackle the sergeant, and was standing, looking very dejected, with his hands in the air, his belongings abandoned on the grass.

"Jim, handcuff our friend here and take him back to the station. I need a word with Mrs Dalton, and then I'll follow you back. Arrest him on suspicion of murder and book him in."

"Right, Sarge."

Jim Dolan placed McCarthy's hands behind his back and fitted the handcuffs while reciting the arrest caution. Peadar Tobin collected the laptop and bag to take them back separately in his own car, while Mulholland replaced his weapon and strolled back to the front door of Christine Dalton's house, where she was standing with tears running down her cheeks.

"That was a bad choice you made, Christine. You knew we were looking for Gerard, but you didn't let us know. It makes him look very guilty, and you may be facing charges, too, for harbouring a suspect and obstructing the Gardaí," Mulholland said.

"But he hasn't done anything, Sergeant. He swore to me, and I believe him."

"That's not what it looks like, Christine. I'm not going to charge you with anything yet, till we see how this works out, but don't go anywhere, will you?"

"Sure, where would I be going, Sergeant? I was only trying to help the lad, and blood's thicker than water," Dalton said.

"As I said, we'll see. Now, I have to go. Has he any other possessions here at all, Christine?"

"No. It's all in that backpack of his, and you have that now."

"Very well. I'll be in touch."

On the way back into Clifden, Mulholland stopped his car in a convenient lay-by at the side of the N59, and called Maureen Lyons in Galway.

"Hello, Maureen. It's Séan. We have Gerard McCarthy in custody now. He was hiding out at his sister's place in Shanakeever. Peadar and Jim are going to book him in and look after him. Do you want to come out to start questioning him?"

"Gosh, well done, Séan. How did you find him?"

"Ah, we have our ways out here in the west, Maureen. It wasn't that hard to figure out. Do you think he's our man for the murder of young Lavelle?"

"It looks very much like it, Séan, but let's not jump the gun. I'll set off in a few minutes with Sally Fahy, and we'll be there in an hour or so. Put the kettle on, and well done, Séan, well done."

* * *

On the way out to Clifden, Lyons asked Fahy what she thought of the state of the case.

"It looks like a slam dunk, boss. The fact that McCarthy ran away after Lavelle was killed kinda stitches him up, doesn't it?"

"It certainly looks that way, Sally. But I'd be cautious about jumping to conclusions. Let's see what he has to say before we make our minds up fully. But I agree, it doesn't look good for him."

The two detectives spent the rest of the journey in thoughtful silence. Lyons was plotting a strategy for the best way to approach the forthcoming interview. She knew McCarthy was a clever young man, so she would have to be on top form if she was to outsmart him. She also had to be careful to manage Fahy's line of questioning. Fahy was brilliant in an action situation, but Lyons wasn't so sure of her interviewing skills. As they sped towards their destination, Lyons wondered if she hadn't made a mistake in bringing Fahy with her. Would she have been better with the more experienced Eamon Flynn? Only time would tell.

Chapter Twenty-nine

Lyons and Fahy breezed into the Clifden Garda station.

"Hi, Séan. How goes it?"

"Ah, 'tis yourself, Maureen. And Sergeant Fahy too. Good day, ladies. I've just put on the kettle. Would you like a cup of tea or coffee?"

Lyons smiled inwardly at her friend and colleague who seemed to have an endless supply of hot beverages on tap around the clock. But she also recognized that Mulholland was rightly feeling a little self-satisfied following recent events.

"Tea for me, Séan. Thanks. What about you, Sally?"

"I'll have a coffee, please. Not too strong and plenty of milk. Thanks."

Séan Mulholland got up from his seat and set about preparing the refreshments. He returned a few minutes later carrying a tray with three mugs and a sizeable plate of chocolate Goldgrain biscuits.

Lyons took up her tea and a biscuit.

"Thanks, Séan. That's just what the doctor ordered. So, tell me – what's the story with yer man?" Lyons said.

Mulholland went on to describe his earlier visit to Shanakeever and the capture of Gerard McCarthy.

"What do you think we should do about the sister, Maureen?"

"Let's see how it goes with himself, then we'll decide. To be honest, based on what you say, I'm not sure there are really grounds for prosecution. But if we find out she's more heavily involved, then that would be a different matter altogether."

"I agree. She's not an evil woman. Far from it, in my view. But as you say, let's see what comes out of your interview," Mulholland said.

"I hope you're going to sit in, Séan. He's your collar after all," Lyons said.

"Ah, now, Maureen. I've done my bit. Wouldn't it be better if I left it to the professionals? Yourself and the sergeant here will have more luck with him. By all accounts, he's a bit of a ladies' man in any case."

Lyons smiled at Fahy. Perhaps they'd just been given the key to unlocking the events of Christmas Eve.

* * *

When Lyons and Fahy entered the rather cold and sparse interview room in Clifden Garda station, Gerard McCarthy was reclining uncomfortably in the polypropylene chair, well back from the table that was bolted to the floor, with his legs spread wide apart. He had a smug grin on his rather childlike face, and he looked anything but the type of murderer that Lyons and Fahy had encountered previously.

Fahy recited the necessary mantra for the recording device, while Lyons appraised the suspect she had in front of her.

"Mr McCarthy, would you like to have a solicitor present for this interview?" Lyons said.

"Do I need one?" McCarthy replied.

"That's entirely up to you, but you have been arrested on a serious charge. You might be best to be represented."

Lyons knew from experience and from the general demeanour of the man that he would decline such assistance.

"No, you're OK. Let's just get on with it," he said. He straightened himself up and leant in, with his elbows on the table.

"OK. Tell me, Mr McCarthy, what line of business are you in?" Lyons said.

"I thought we were here to talk about the incident out at Kingstown on Christmas Eve. What business is it of yours what I do for a living?"

"Just answer the question, please," Lyons said coolly.

McCarthy stared at Maureen Lyons, hoping to intimidate her with his cold blue eyes.

"I'm a data analyst," he said eventually.

Fahy decided to intervene.

"Can you describe what exactly that entails please, Mr McCarthy?" she said.

"It entails analysing data," he said, smirking.

"And what data would that be?" Fahy persisted.

"Just lots of stuff I get sent from all over. You wouldn't understand, love."

"I'm not your love, Mr McCarthy, and I'll trust you to bear that in mind. I'm a police officer investigating a very serious crime and you'd do well to remember that," Fahy retorted.

McCarthy let his eyes wander to the ceiling.

"Whatever," he said nonchalantly.

It was Lyons' turn to take over.

"Where were you on the night of Christmas Eve last?" Lyons said.

"You know this already. I was in my mobile home out at Kingstown, working."

"All evening?"

"Yes. Christmas is a time when a mass of data gets generated from the companies I work with. I had to collect it all and forward it to my main processing centre before 2 a.m., so that the results would be ready the following day. Mine is a 24/7/365 operation."

"Would that be the mainframe at the university, Mr McCarthy?" Fahy said.

"My, my. You are well informed."

"So, tell me, did you have any callers on Christmas Eve when you were working at home?" Lyons asked.

"Yes, I did as a matter of fact. And old mate dropped in to see me for a few minutes, but he didn't stay long."

"What was this old mate's name?" Lyons said.

"Lavelle, Jack Lavelle. We were in college together a few years back."

"And what did Jack Lavelle want, apart from wishing you a happy Christmas?" Lyons said.

"Nothing much really. He just wanted to catch up."

"How did he get there? It's not exactly on a bus route."

"I dunno. He just appeared. Maybe he had a car out on the road or something."

"Was that not a bit odd, Mr McCarthy? After all, it's a funny time to be doing house calls, don't you think?" Fahy said.

"That was Jack all over. Very unpredictable. Very spontaneous."

"How long did he stay?" Fahy asked.

"Not long. He had things to do, places to go."

"Did you have a drink together, given the occasion?" Fahy asked.

"No, no. We didn't. To be honest I was keen to get on with my work, so I wasn't terribly hospitable. Time and tide wait for no man, after all."

Lyons took over again.

"Indeed. What time was it when Lavelle left your place?" she asked.

"I'm not sure. Not that late. Maybe 10 p.m. or thereabouts."

"And how do you think he ended up dead in the ditch just outside your mobile home?"

"Who knows? I've been trying to figure that out. Maybe he tripped in the dark and hit his head on a rock or something. Yes, that's probably it," McCarthy said.

"When did you realize he had come to grief?" Lyons said.

"I saw the body early on Christmas Day. I panicked. I knew you lot would think I had something to do with it. I didn't know what to do. So, I took off."

"And you never thought to call the Gardaí or even an ambulance for your friend?"

"I knew he was beyond help, so what was the point?" McCarthy said.

"Still, you must have known that the matter needed to be reported," Lyons said.

"I told you. I panicked."

"Where did you spend Christmas Day?" Lyons said.

"I snuck into the university and slept on the floor of the computer room. I have access to it for my work."

"How long did you spend there?" Lyons asked.

"A few nights. Then I went to Christine's."

"So, just to be clear, are you saying that the last time you saw Jack Lavelle alive was when he left your caravan at Kingstown and at that time he was perfectly all right?" Lyons said.

"Yes. That's exactly what I'm saying, Inspector."

Lyons and Fahy exchanged glances.

"Mr McCarthy, we have a witness that says there was an altercation between you and Jack Lavelle that night. What have you to say about that?" Lyons said.

"That's my business. No comment," McCarthy said.

"But I'm sure you can see that it could be relevant to our enquiries. After all, if you and he fought, and he ended up dead, well, you can see the implication," Lyons said.

"I told you. He was perfectly all right when he left my place."

Fahy took up the questioning.

"What was the altercation about?" Fahy asked.

"That's my business."

Lyons decided they needed a break.

"OK. Let's take a break for an hour or so. Sally, can you see that Mr McCarthy is escorted back to his cell. I'll be with Séan."

Chapter Thirty

"What do you think, Sally?" Lyons said.

She was sitting in the main office in Clifden Garda station with Séan Mulholland, who was, inevitably, enjoying yet another cup of tea.

"I think we have a problem. If he sticks to that story, we have bugger all to go on. Apart from the tiny bloodstain on the caravan door frame, and the fact that he scarpered, but that's nothing like enough to get a conviction. The whole thing is very circumstantial. Any ideas?" Fahy said.

"Well, we can't just do nothing," Lyons said.

Lyons remained silent for several minutes, thinking, before saying to Fahy, "Something is telling me that this whole thing just isn't right. I think there's more to it than we know just now. And all this crap about data has me bothered too. We need to turn up the heat. Look, can you get onto Eamon? Get him to bring in Sandra Ward for another chat. Ask him to make a bit of a fuss about it. You know, squad car at her place of employment with blue lights, etc. Then get him to get bank records for all the actors in the whole thing. And I'm not happy about the professor either. But he's a canny old duffer. We might have more luck with Ursula Kenny. When I've had a good go at Ward, we might have another chat with Kenny."

"Right, boss. And are we going back to town then?" Fahy said.

"Yes, we are," Lyons said.

"What about McCarthy?" Mulholland asked.

"How long have we got him for, Séan?" Lyons said.

"Just till the end of the day, unless you want me to look for an extension."

"No, that won't be necessary. Release him on police bail pending further enquiries. Get his passport, and tell him he has to stay within the county. Tell him if he doesn't comply it will go badly for his sister," Lyons said.

"That's not strictly speaking true, is it, Maureen?" Mulholland said.

"No, it isn't, but he doesn't know that, does he?"

"Fair enough. God, you haven't lost your touch," Mulholland said, smiling.

"I'll take that as a compliment, Séan, and you're not doing too badly yourself."

On the way back to Galway, Lyons called her friend and colleague Sinéad Loughran on her mobile phone.

"Hi, Sinéad. Listen, I want you to do something for me. Can you get a team back out to Kingstown where Lavelle's body was found? We've missed something, and I need to find it."

"Hmm… OK. What do you think we've missed, Maureen?"

"If I knew that, I would be asking you, Sinéad. But we've missed something, that's for sure. Can you organize it?"

"Yes, of course. I'll get going on it now, although I'd rather not be out there in the dark. Will it do first thing tomorrow?" Loughran said.

"Yes, of course. And you'd better let Sergeant Mulholland know what you're up to. It's his patch after all."

"Yes, OK. Will do. I'll call you if we find anything."

* * *

Sandra Ward wasn't at all happy. Flynn had done as Sally Fahy had asked and driven out to Ward's workplace. Fortunately, she was in the showroom, but she was very indignant at being removed in full view of her colleagues.

Flynn had provided her with tea in the interview room while they waited for Lyons to arrive back from Clifden. But there was no conversation. Ward was fuming silently at her plight.

As soon as Lyons entered the room, Ward let fly. She stood up aggressively, waving her arms.

"What the bloody hell do you think you're doing, Inspector? I could lose my job over this, and I haven't done anything," she barked. Her face was very red and her eyes glaring.

"Calm down, Ms Ward. The sooner you can answer my questions, the sooner you'll be out of here, and we'll drive you back when we're done. I'd like you to recount the events of Christmas Eve for us. Start from when and where you picked up Jack Lavelle to take him out to Kingstown."

"I already told you all this. I just gave him a lift. He called me the previous day and said he had to go and see Gerard, but had no way of getting there. He asked me if I'd take him there. I told him that we were finishing up at around 4 p.m. in the office and that I could drive him out after that when I'd had something to eat. I picked him up in town at soon after 7 p.m. and off we went."

"Had you ever done anything like this for Lavelle before?"

"No, of course not."

"Then why would you go to all that trouble on Christmas Eve of all days? Were you in a relationship with Lavelle?"

"No, I was not. He was just a friend, and I was doing him a favour, that's all."

"But you told us previously that you didn't know Lavelle. Why did you lie?"

"I didn't want to get involved."

"There must have been more to it than that, Sandra. Why don't you tell me the rest of it?" Lyons said.

Ward looked down to the floor, before lifting her head and staring Lyons in the face.

"All right. There was a bit more to it. Jack said that McCarthy owed him money. A lot of money. And he knew that he kept a good deal of cash out at the site to pay the builders and suppliers and so on. He told me that he would collect a few grand from Gerard, and that he'd pay me handsomely for my trouble. So, I went along with it. I earn most of my money at work on commission, and things have been a bit difficult lately what with Covid and all, so I needed some extra to pay for Christmas."

"Did Lavelle indicate how much he would pay you?"

"He said a few hundred."

"I see. And did you collect?"

"No. When I saw that Jack and Gerard were getting into some kind of heated argument, I took off. I didn't like the look of the way it was going, and I didn't want to be any part of it."

"Do you think McCarthy killed Lavelle?" Lyons said.

"Don't you?" Ward said.

"Do you know why Lavelle thought McCarthy owed him money?"

"No, well not really. It was something to do with McCarthy's work, but I don't know the details."

"Neither of them confided in you, then?" Lyons said.

"No, they didn't."

"And are you certain that the last time you saw Lavelle, he was OK? You didn't see Gerard McCarthy striking him or anything?"

"No. I told you. I got the hell out."

Lyons remained silent for several minutes. She was trying to figure out if they could legitimately hold on to the woman. In the end, she said, "All right, Ms Ward. You can go. But we may need to talk to you again. I take it you have no plans to leave the country?"

"As if," Ward said.

Chapter Thirty-one

The next morning, first thing, Sinéad Loughran organized three other forensic officers to travel out to Kingstown with her in her enormous white 4x4. She decided that they would all travel in the same vehicle to minimize contamination of the scene.

As soon as they were underway, Loughran called Clifden Garda station. The call was answered by Mulholland.

"Hello, Sergeant, it's Sinéad Loughran here. Inspector Lyons has asked me to revisit the site of the Lavelle killing to have another good look around. I thought I'd better let you know," she said.

"Oh, right. Well, if you don't mind, Sinéad, I'd like to be there when you carry out your examination. Where are you now?" Mulholland said.

"We're just coming into Oughterard. I'm guessing we'll be at Kingstown in about another fifty minutes or so. Do you want us to stop in Clifden, or will we meet you there?"

"Let's meet at the site. I'll bring Jim Dolan out with me, and we can manage the traffic, if there is any, while you do your thing."

"Righto, Sergeant. See you in a while."

Mulholland calculated he'd have just enough time for a cup of tea before he set off out west with Dolan.

* * *

The weather was beginning to close in as Loughran approached the site where Lavelle had been found. While the location was very remote, Loughran could see the attraction of the site with its uninterrupted view of the white strand and the island just offshore. There was a stiff breeze blowing in from the Atlantic Ocean, and heavy grey clouds were approaching, signalling the imminent arrival of heavy rain. As Loughran pulled the jeep up short, parking half up on the grass verge, behind the brightly coloured squad car occupied by Mulholland and Dolan, the first few spots of water landed on the windscreen.

"Right, team, let's don our crime scene suits before we start. We'll split into two teams. You two, work the hedgerows just inside the plot where Lavelle was found," she said, nodding to two of the young men seated in the rear of her vehicle.

"We'll concentrate on the verges and bushes out here on the road."

They all got out of the jeep, putting on the white suits and drawing the hoods over their heads to protect against the rain. Loughran walked towards the Garda car, and spoke to Mulholland.

"Good morning, Sergeant. Is there anything you want us to do specifically?" Loughran said.

"Ah, no, you're grand. You just carry on as you were, but let me know if you find anything useful. We'll stay here and look out for any vehicles that come along and direct them away from you."

Loughran wasn't quite sure why Mulholland felt that his presence was needed, but she surmised that he felt a little possessive about the case, and perhaps a bit territorial about the area. This had been his patch for more than thirty years, after all.

Loughran and her colleague worked their way along by the rough grass at the side of the road, poking the ground with their long aluminium sticks. The rain was more persistent now, and they were all feeling a bit miserable about their situation.

When they had been searching for almost half an hour, the man working with Loughran shouted back to her.

"Sinéad, I'm just going further on down here a bit. I need to relieve myself."

"OK, Tommy. I promise I won't look!" Loughran said, smiling.

Tommy Boyle walked on down the road for about fifty metres and found a tall gorse bush to conceal him as he did his business. When he had finished, and was coming back to the search area through the rough grass, he almost tripped over something half buried in the weeds. He bent down to see what it was, and when he saw the item lying hidden in the undergrowth, he let out a shout.

"Over here, boss! I've found something."

Loughran strode across to where her colleague was standing. Boyle bent down and carefully lifted a short metal bar with a bend at one end between his gloved forefinger and thumb.

"Looks like a wheel brace to me, boss," he said.

"So it does, Tommy. And although it's started to rust a bit, that doesn't look like rust on the blunt end. Give it here. I'll bag it up."

Loughran took her prize back, stopping at the squad car where Mulholland and Dolan were now sheltering from the rain.

"One of the lads found this over there by that clump of bushes. Looks like it was thrown away by someone. I think that may be blood on the end of it. I'll get it back to the lab later and let you know. I don't think there's much point in us battling the elements here for much longer, Sergeant. What do you think?"

"Whatever you say, Sinéad. But that was a good find," Mulholland said. "I think Jim and I will head back now too. There's no one about. Thanks, Sinéad. We'll talk later."

* * *

Lyons was having a difficult morning. Soon after she arrived at the station, her office phone sprang to life. It was Hays.

"Hi, Mick. What's up?" she said.

"You're not going to like this. I'm sorry, but Plunkett has been on to me, and it's not like him to be at it so early," Hays said.

"What's bothering him?"

"You are. He's had a call from the president of UCG. Apparently, you've been harassing a Professor Madden, and they'd like it to stop."

"Ah, excellent. So, we've rattled a few cages then. That's progress of a kind. Oh, and by the way, I'm not finished yet. There's something going on out there that I'm not happy about. I presume you didn't call to warn me off, Mick?"

"As if that would make any difference! No, I didn't. But for heaven's sake, be careful, hun. The university has a lot of influence in this city, and of course they have friends in high places, so don't go crashing around like a bull in a china shop," Hays said.

"Now, Mick. How long have you known me? Have I ever upset anyone badly enough to cause a rumpus? Now honestly, have I?"

"Yes, you have. Lots of times. And that's one of the reasons why you always get results. So, anyway, I've delivered the message. Over to you now."

"Thanks, Mick, I think. Catch you later."

Lyons didn't respond well to this kind of intervention. She hated political interference of any kind into police work. It rarely achieved anything, other than to prolong an investigation, and sometimes such meddling could allow a criminal time to escape justice.

"Now I know there's something worth digging into out there," she said to herself. She grabbed her jacket from the back of the chair, and left her office.

Out in the open-plan, Sally Fahy was relaxing with a cup of instant coffee.

"C'mon, Sally. You're with me. We're going to cause some trouble!"

On the drive out to the university campus, Lyons filled her colleague in on the conversation she had had with Superintendent Hays.

"What do you reckon, Sally?"

"Cripes, boss. You do believe in living dangerously, don't you?"

"No, it's not that. In my experience, every single time you get an intervention of that kind in a case, there's something seriously fishy going on. Otherwise, why bother?" Lyons said.

"I see what you mean. But what could it be? It's a flipping college, for God's sake. Hardly a den of skulduggery."

"That's what we need to find out. I reckon Ursula Kenny is the best source. When we get there, I'd like you to go and fetch her on some pretext. Try not to let Madden know we are here. Bring her down to the café for a wee chat."

"OK. Mine's a skinny latte, by the way," Fahy said.

"And a bun, no doubt."

"Of course!"

Chapter Thirty-two

Lyons was sitting in the café at the university when Fahy came bouncing in.

"Hi. Where's Ursula?" Lyons said.

"She hasn't turned up for work today. And she hasn't called in either. I spoke to Madden. He says it's completely out of character. He doesn't know what's going on," Fahy said.

"OK. Well, we need to get her home address. You stay here and have your coffee. I'll go and find someone that can tell us where she lives."

Fortunately, the university had gone to the trouble of providing clear signage all around the maze of corridors, and it didn't take Lyons long to locate the administration office for the IT building. She entered the spacious area, crowded with desks, PCs and quite a few people, and spoke to the first person she came across.

Having introduced herself by showing her warrant card, she said, "I need to get a home address for Ursula Kenny."

"I'm not sure we can give out that information, Inspector."

"Look. I'm not here for fun. Your employee Ursula Kenny may be in serious danger. And I mean, life-or-death danger. And while I'm at it, we need to speak to her in connection with an ongoing murder enquiry. So, if you still want to hold out on me, that's fine, but I hope you are prepared to face the consequences."

The woman she had been speaking to stared at her for a moment, and then turned on her heels, went to a filing cabinet, and withdrew a file. She came back to where Lyons was standing and handed it to her.

Lyons made a note of the address, and closed the file, handing it back to the woman. She said nothing, but left to rejoin her colleague.

* * *

Ursula Kenny rented a room in a family house on Newcastle Park. It was very convenient for the university – just a few minutes' walk – which is why she favoured it, even if it could be a little awkward from time to time if she wanted to bring anyone home.

Lyons and Fahy got back into the car, and set off for Kenny's address.

When they arrived, they both got out of the car and approached the front of the property. Lyons rapped three times on the glass-panelled door, and stood back. There was no response.

"Sally, see if you can get around the back and have a look. There may be another way in."

Lyons stepped up to the front door and knocked again, this time quite a bit more forcefully. But the response was the same. Then she heard a shout coming from the back of the house.

"Boss, 'round here."

Lyons walked around to the rear of the property to find Fahy standing outside the open back door.

"Don't hang about, Sally. Get in," Lyons said.

The house was in very good condition. The back door opened into a modern kitchen with pale green fitted units, modern appliances, and a small round kitchen table and chairs that looked as if they might have come from IKEA. A door led off the kitchen to the hallway.

Lyons shouted Kenny's name.

"Ursula, it's the police. Are you here?"

There was no reply.

Lyons looked in the two rooms off the hallway, and found them empty. She then gestured to Fahy to go upstairs, and kept calling out as Fahy ascended, followed by herself. At the top of the stairs there were four doors off the landing. Three of the doors stood open, but one was closed. Lyons approached that door and knocked.

"Ursula, are you in there?" she said.

When there was no response, she tried the handle and the door opened easily. Inside, Ursula Kenny lay on her stomach, fully clothed, on the only bed in the room. Beside her on the bedside locker was a bottle of vodka, one-third full, and scattered on the bed and the floor were blister packs of tablets, with one or two of the little while pills dotted around the unmoving form of the young woman.

"Jesus!" exclaimed Lyons. "Quick! Call an ambulance. I'll see if I can rouse her."

Fahy did as she was instructed, telling the call centre that there was a suspected overdose, and asking them to expedite the ambulance.

Lyons turned Kenny onto her side, and tried to wake her, but the woman was out cold, though, mercifully, still breathing in short, shallow breaths.

"What's she taken, Sally?"

Fahy lifted one of the empty blister packs from the floor.

"Looks like nitrazepam. I wonder how many she's swallowed?" Fahy said.

"God knows."

As Lyons tried in vain to wake Kenny from her stupor, she could hear the sirens from the ambulance approaching.

"Go down and let them in the front door, Sally. Tell them what she's taken too," Lyons said.

A few minutes later, Lyons could hear the heavy footsteps of the paramedics coming up the stairs. First into the room was a young man in a green jumpsuit, carrying a sizeable piece of kit. He was quickly followed by a young woman in a similar outfit.

The paramedic leaned over Ursula Kenny and pulled back her eyelids. Her eyes were partially rolled back. He placed a finger at the side of her neck, and said to his colleague, "She's breathing, but the pulse is weak. Let's give her some oxygen and get her out of here."

The female paramedic took out a small grey cylinder with a clear plastic pipe and a face mask attached. She placed the mask over Kenny's face, and opened the valve on the cylinder with a distinctive hiss. Then the male paramedic scooped Kenny up in his arms, and the three of them made their way awkwardly out of the room and down the stairs.

"Go with them, Sally. Bring the empty tablet package too. Stay close. We need to talk to her as soon as she comes around."

"OK, boss. I'll call you when I have any news," Fahy said.

Once outside, the paramedics placed Kenny in the ambulance and strapped her to the narrow bed. The female paramedic unfolded a seat beside the patient, and hooked her up to some monitoring equipment, while Fahy sat on the other bench in the back of the ambulance. The man closed up the rear doors of the vehicle, got back into the driving seat, and set off with sirens blaring and blue lights flashing.

Chapter Thirty-three

Back at the Garda station, Lyons tried to settle into her work, but the thoughts of Ursula Kenny, possibly near death following what looked like a suicide attempt, kept drifting into her head.

She got up and went outside to find Eamon Flynn and John O'Connor. She explained what they had found at Ursula Kenny's house, and told them that Sally Fahy would be remaining at the hospital for the rest of the day.

"Right, folks. What have we discovered from digging into McCarthy's bank account?" she said.

"It's a very strange arrangement, boss. Firstly, he has three different accounts. There's money flowing between them all at times, and lots of cash going out and even more coming in," Flynn said.

"How much cash has he between the three accounts?" Lyons asked.

Flynn reached for a sheet of paper.

"The total is €180,000 and change, but I don't think that's the extent of it. It looks as if he has some overseas bank accounts too, possibly in Germany or Switzerland. We are just checking the IBAN codes now," he said.

"OK. Well, first I'd like to find out where his money is coming from. Can you trace any of the lodgements?" Lyons said.

John O'Connor raised his hand.

"Yes, John," Lyons said.

"There's something else, boss. I need to check a bit further, but it looks like he's been transferring money to both Sandra Ward and Ursula Kenny. Their accounts are held locally. And he pays the university a fixed monthly amount, and there's a regular monthly withdrawal in cash too."

"OK, well, stay on it, John, but what about the lodgements?"

"Oh, sorry, yes. There are several transfers in US dollars every month from Citibank and J P Morgan. These are quite big amounts. And it looks as if he has a crypto account too, but I can't get into that," O'Connor said.

"Do any of these payments correspond to any files on his laptop?" Lyons said.

"Yes, they do. The dollar receipts are in payment for invoices he has issued to a number of US companies. The work is described as data analysis in each case. But there's nothing on the laptop about the rest. But he has been on some pretty dodgy websites. His browser history was quite revealing," O'Connor said.

"OK. Look, can you two keep digging? Look for patterns. Try and see what the source of the non-US payments are. And tot up how much Ward and Kenny have been paid over, say, the past year. Is there any sign of Lavelle anywhere in terms of money transfers or correspondence?" Lyons said.

"No, boss. But there are some emails that Lavelle sent, but they don't seem to have been replied to," O'Connor said.

"Any theme you can discern?"

"Not really. Just things like 'we need to talk', 'when can we meet?', that sort of thing."

"OK. Thanks, guys. Let's get together later in the day to catch up. Oh, and I know it's New Year's Day tomorrow, but we'll have to come in, I'm afraid," Lyons said.

Surprisingly, the announcement was not met with groans from the team.

* * *

Towards the end of the working day, Lyons received a call from Fahy who was still at the hospital.

"Hi, Sally. What's the story?"

"She's going to be OK, boss. They got her in time and pumped her out before all the tranquilizer was absorbed. She's pretty woozy, but she's awake, sort of," Fahy said.

"A little too much information there, Sally! But when can we talk to her?"

"The doctor says they want to try and get a little food into her to restart her digestive system. But we might be able to have a few minutes with her after that, say, seven o'clock or so," Fahy said.

"Hmm… look, the poor girl has had a rough day. Why don't we leave it till first thing tomorrow? We'll get more out of her then anyway. But listen, I want you to organize a uniformed Garda outside her room for the night. Can you do that?" Lyons said.

"Yes, of course, but do you think she's in danger?"

"I don't know. But I'm not taking any chances. When you have that set up, you get off home. I'll see you here early doors. I'm afraid we all have to work tomorrow, sorry."

"That's fine, boss, I have no mad plans anyway. I hate New Year's Eve! Any other news?"

"Nothing important. I'll bring you up to date tomorrow."

"OK. Thanks. See you."

* * *

Lyons was frustrated at the apparent lack of progress. The case appeared to be developing in front of their eyes, but they couldn't see the wood for the trees. When she felt like this, there was only one solution. She called upstairs.

"Hi, Mick. It's me. I don't suppose you have a few minutes?"

From the tone of her voice, Hays recognized the nature of the call.

"Give me fifteen, then I'm all yours. Do you want to go and grab some grub?" Hays said.

"Sounds like a plan. I'll book somewhere, though all the restaurants could be full this evening."

"Ah, don't worry, O'Connaire's will squeeze us in, I'm sure."

"OK. See you at the front door in fifteen minutes."

Lyons called O'Connaire's, down at the docks, and managed to get a table for them, and then went to the bathroom to comb her hair and check that her makeup was holding up, and that she looked respectable.

They drove in Hays' car to the quayside and found parking easily, though Hays had to go to a machine to buy a ticket, as the chargeable hours were still in force.

Inside the restaurant they were shown to their favourite table in the window overlooking the harbour. The sea looked grey and grim, but inside was warm and welcoming, and they selected their food before opening up the subject that both of them knew Lyons was anxious about.

"So, what's up, Maureen?" Hays said.

"Ah, the usual. The case is doing my head in. One dead guy, lots of suspects, and very few decent leads," Lyons said.

Hays smiled.

"It's never easy, is it? What happened to the days when we found the killer standing over his victim with a knife in his hand dripping with fresh blood?"

"We never did, Mick, as you well know."

"Yeah, but these cases seem to be getting more and more obscure as time goes by. I mean to say, university dons, computer operators, data analysts, interior designers – it's a bloody nightmare," Hays said.

"So, you have been following the case, then, Superintendent?"

Lyons gave her partner a withering look. The moment was saved by the arrival of the food which looked, as always, sumptuous.

"Guilty as charged, Inspector. You know I have to keep abreast of this stuff, and especially now that Plunkett is getting it in the ear over the university involvement. And you know we have to be very careful with anything to do with these foreign direct investment companies too. They contribute massively to our economy, and no one wants to see them embroiled in something unsavoury. Kid gloves, Detective Lyons, kid gloves."

"That's all very well. But tell that to Jack Lavelle's parents. They just want to know what happened to their son, and why," Lyons said.

"OK. So have you followed the Mick Hays first principle of crime detection?"

"You mean, follow the money?"

"I do. These things are usually about love or money or both, and I don't see much love in the situation, not so far, anyway," Hays said.

"Me neither. We are trying to follow the money, but it's bitch hard. There are bank accounts literally all over the world, and cash flying in all directions."

"And who benefits, mostly?"

"I'd say Gerard McCarthy, from what we can tell. But I have no actual evidence against the man. Nothing that would get past the DPP anyway."

Hays said nothing. He finished his food, parked his knife and fork, and pushed his plate a little bit away from him.

"OK, well, listen, I'm sorry about this, but I have to level with you. Plunkett is getting very jumpy. He's had 'the call' from Merrion Street in Dublin. Professor Madden is, apparently, well connected. Plunkett has asked me if you're the right woman for the job, given the political sensitivities. I think your diplomatic credentials are a bit tarnished with the powers that be."

"Bloody cheek! I'll give them diplomatic credentials! For fuck's sake, Mick, what's going on?" Lyons said.

"I'm honestly not sure, but it's heavy."

"What do you suggest?" Lyons said.

"Look, hun, I'm not going to tell you what to do. You're a big girl, and probably much better at all of this than I am at this stage. But maybe if you took it easy on Madden and his lot, and focused elsewhere for a while, they might ease off the political pressure."

"Hmm… not easy to do with Ursula Kenny in hospital following a suicide attempt," Lyons said.

"And you're sure that's what it was? Suicide, I mean?" Hays said.

"Jesus, Mick. Stop, will ye! You're frying what's left of my brain!"

Chapter Thirty-four

When Lyons arrived at the station the following morning, she was just as agitated as she had been in the restaurant. There was a message for her to call Sinéad Loughran, who had also agreed to come to work on the bank holiday, and she dearly hoped that Loughran would have some good news for her.

"Hi, Sinéad. It's me. You were looking for me."

"Oh, hi, Maureen. Yes, I was. You know that implement we brought back from Kingstown yesterday?"

"You mean the wheel brace or whatever?"

"Yes. Well, I was right. It has traces of blood and hair on it, and they match Lavelle, so it looks as if that could be the murder weapon," Loughran said.

"Nice one, Sinéad. But listen, would something that small be able to inflict that much damage? The guy's head was mush."

"Oh, yes, for sure. And the main indentation in Jack Lavelle's skull fits it perfectly. I think you'll find that it's the murder weapon, all right."

"Cool. Any fingerprints on it?" Lyons said.

"Yes. Just Sandra Ward's."

"But why on earth would Ward want to terminate Lavelle? It doesn't make any sense. Where's the motive?"

"That's for you to figure out, Maureen. I'm just a humble forensics person. You're the detective," Loughran said.

"Thanks a bunch. OK, I'd best get on. This changes just about all our thinking. But thanks anyway, I think!"

"Bye. See ya," Loughran said, hanging up.

Lyons wasted no time in bringing Fahy and Flynn up to date.

"Obviously, we need to talk to Sandra Ward as a matter of urgency. Eamon, can you and Sally go out and bring her in. Arrest her this time on suspicion of murder, and read her rights. I'll get the evidence back from Sinéad, and we'll confront her. In the meantime, if anyone can figure out why on earth she might want to bump Jack Lavelle off, please don't hold back."

"Right, boss," Flynn said.

Fahy was already getting her jacket on.

* * *

When Lyons and Flynn came into the interview room, Sandra Ward was seated beside her sombre-looking solicitor, Martin Gilhooly.

Lyons sat down opposite them, and recited the necessary short speech for the recording device.

"Well, Sandra, do you know why you are here?"

Gilhooly interjected.

"Inspector, this is the second time you have hauled my client away in a squad car. And is all this really necessary on New Year's Day? It's really not good enough."

Lyons ignored the man's indignant outburst.

"Ms Ward, we have recovered a wheel brace from the scene of Jack Lavelle's killing. The item seems to fit the tool kit in your car, and it has Lavelle's blood and hair on it, and your fingerprints, but no others. Can you explain please?" Lyons said.

Ward looked at Gilhooly who remained poker-faced.

"Not really, no. How do you know that came from my car?" Ward said, rather feebly.

"I'll ask the questions, if you don't mind. And unless you have a sensible explanation for what I have described, you'll be charged with murder within the next half-hour," Lyons said. She was in no mood to be messed about.

Ward looked plaintively at Gilhooly, but got no response. He stared at her for a long moment, and then, as if being woken from a daydream, jerked his head and said, "Inspector, I need some time to confer with my client."

Lyons looked at Flynn.

"Very well. You have fifteen minutes, and I presume you will be advising your client to tell the truth about these matters."

Lyons nodded to Flynn, and they both got up and left the room.

Outside, Lyons said to her colleague, "What do you reckon, Eamon?"

"I'd say she's banged to rights. They'll be seeing if they can twist it around to look like some kind of terrible accident or maybe manslaughter."

"We'll see about that!"

* * *

Lyons and Flynn were back in the interview room fifteen minutes later. Lyons didn't want to give Ward and Gilhooly too much time to concoct a story.

"Well," Lyons said, "I'm waiting."

Ward took a deep breath before replying.

"It goes back to when we were all in college. Jack and I were lovers. I thought it was a forever thing. I was completely mad about him. Totally smitten. When we left college, I was still very much in love with him, but I discovered he had been unfaithful. It was some Indian woman he met at work. Samira is her name. He and I parted company, but I never got over it. I was still in love with him, poor fool me."

"What was McCarthy's part in all of this?" Flynn said.

"Jack and Gerard were good mates in college. They worked on some new-fangled software system for analysing data. Jack thought they were partners, but when McCarthy started to make money from it – real money – he cut Jack off. He didn't give him anything. Jack was in a menial job and was constantly broke, so he decided to confront McCarthy who obviously was getting rich fast on the back of whatever they had created together."

"Go on," Lyons said.

"Jack called me on Christmas Eve and said he had to go out and see McCarthy to get some money out of him. He told me McCarthy owed him thousands, and if I would drive him out to Kingstown, he'd pay me handsomely. Because, I guess, I still had feelings for Jack, I agreed," Ward said.

"How did the false plates get onto the car?" Lyons said.

"That was Jack's idea. He supplied them and stuck them on over the real ones. He said it was in case it got rough out there. Little did he know! After the thing with the wheel, I stopped on the way back to the city, took off the false plates, and dumped them at the side of the road."

"What went wrong out at Kingstown?" Flynn asked.

"All the way out in the bloody car he kept going on and on about Samira. Samira this, Samira that. How happy she made him. He wouldn't shut up. He didn't seem to realize what effect it was having on me. I was getting angrier and angrier."

"So, what happened?" Lyons said.

"I saw him arguing with McCarthy. I was sitting in the car waiting for him to come back with loads of cash. But he got nothing. He said Samira would be disappointed because he had promised her the air fare to go back and see her family in Delhi. I just lost it. The red mist descended. The wheel brace was in the side pocket of the driver's door, and I grabbed it and whacked him all about the head and face. I completely lost control. He collapsed on the rough ground, and I rolled him into the ditch under the gorse bushes. Then I went back onto the road and threw the wheel brace as far as I could into the undergrowth."

"Did you know he was dead?" Flynn asked.

"No, no of course not. I thought he'd just have a sore head the next day. I drove back to Galway, but I was crying and couldn't see the road properly through my tears and I hit a fence or something, bursting the tyre. That's when I called on Tadgh Deasy."

"Did Gerard McCarthy see what happened?" Flynn asked.

"I don't know. I don't think so, but I can't be sure."

"So, just to be clear, you are admitting to striking Jack Lavelle with the wheel brace from your car on the head on Christmas Eve night at Kingstown, causing him to lose his life?" Lyons said.

"I suppose so, but I didn't mean to kill him, I swear."

"OK. Eamon, will you deal with the formalities? Charge Ms Ward with murder and ask her to sign a statement. We'll get her before Judge Meehan tomorrow, assuming he will agree to a special sitting. Will you be asking for bail, Mr Gilhooly?" Lyons said.

"Yes, of course," the solicitor said. "Will you oppose?"

"No, I don't think so, as long as your client surrenders her passport and agrees to present herself twice a week here at Mill Street."

"Thank you," the solicitor said in an unusually cordial tone.

Chapter Thirty-five

Lyons was seated in one of their favourite restaurants for a quick bite with Mick Hays at lunchtime that day. An Béal Bocht, which translated from Gaelic means 'the poor mouth', served delicious meals throughout the day, and being well known in the establishment, Hays and Lyons always got served quickly by Liam, the manager.

"So, Mick, any word from Plunkett about that Limerick thing?" Lyons said.

"Hmm… I'm almost afraid to tell you, but it is sorted."

"Go on," Lyons said, looking suspiciously at her partner.

"Well, he told me he had to tell the bosses up in Dublin that he didn't think this new crack unit should be headed up by a woman. I know it's completely inappropriate for lots of reasons, but he said it was the only way he could get you out of it without damaging your excellent reputation," Hays said, between mouthfuls of piping-hot freshly baked lasagna and garlic bread.

"Bloody hell! I don't know whether to laugh or get annoyed. But I have to hand it to him, he's a wily old geezer all the same."

"I think there's a bit more to it, too," Hays said.

"Yeah?"

"Yes. I don't think he wants to lose you from here. I mean just look at your latest triumph. No one else could have solved that the way you did. It was bloody brilliant! And Plunkett knows it only too well, even though he'd never say anything directly to you."

"Hmm… maybe. But unfortunately, it's not all over yet. And he may not like what comes next," Lyons said.

"Oh. Do tell."

"Nope. Need-to-know basis only, Superintendent, I'm afraid."

Hays smiled.

"Now, hurry up and finish your food. I have to get back," Lyons said.

"Yes, ma'am!"

* * *

Back at the station, Lyons gathered the entire team around her.

"Right, everyone, thinking caps on. I know we've solved the unlawful killing of Jack Lavelle, but there are a lot of loose ends we need to tie up."

"Such as?" Sally Fahy said.

"Well, for starters, there's that woman out in Clifden who withheld information about her brother, Gerard McCarthy. That impeded the investigation quite a bit. Then there's Ursula Kenny's attempted suicide. We need to find out what all that was about, and if there's anything we need to do there. And finally, there's McCarthy's side hustle which we can't just ignore. But that one is very sensitive. It's all to do with the many foreign direct investment operations here in Ireland, and not upsetting them it seems. But I'm not having some young fella making loose and free with the data protection regulations for financial gain on our patch. That wouldn't do any of them any good in the long run," Lyons said.

"So, what's the plan then?" Flynn said.

"Sally, you spent quite a bit of time with Kenny when she was in hospital. Do you think you built some kind of rapport?" Lyons said.

"Yes, I guess so," Fahy said.

"Right. Well, I'd like you to go and see her. Find out why she felt it necessary to try and end her life. Spend more time with her. As much as is necessary, but dig a bit too. She'll be feeling sheepish after what happened."

"Right, boss."

"Eamon, will you take on McCarthy? I want to know if what Sandra Ward told us about McCarthy owing Lavelle money is true. Push him a bit if you have to. I'm sure we can dream up a few charges if necessary in order to bring him to heel."

"OK. What about Madden?" Flynn said.

"All in good time, Eamon. We'll get around to him when we know the whole story, but for now, we have to tread carefully. Professor Madden is, apparently, well connected," Lyons said.

"What are you going to do, boss?" Fahy said.

"I'm going to drive out to Clifden and talk to Séan Mulholland about Christine Dalton. I'd like to bring him fully up to date on the whole affair anyway. And I'd prefer to do that face to face."

* * *

The drive out to Clifden, through Moycullen, Oughterard and then up onto the heathland that marked the start of the true Connemara was a cheerless affair. Heavy, solid grey clouds hung over the entire area, and Lyons predicted it wouldn't be long before persistent rain began. She wasn't disappointed. As she sped through Maam Cross on the deserted road, her windscreen wipers were pressed into service, and the accompanying wind started to buffet the car. When she arrived at the Garda station in Clifden, she had to make a dash indoors to avoid getting soaked.

Sergeant Séan Mulholland was sitting at his desk in the office behind the public area of the station. He appeared to be relaxed, with his uniform jacket unbuttoned, but for once he didn't seem to have a mug of tea on the go.

"Ah, Maureen. I wasn't expecting you. Happy New Year to you. Come in and sit you down. Would you like a cup of tea? Peadar is just about to put the kettle on."

"Thanks, Séan, that would be lovely. Many happy returns. It sure knows how to rain in these parts once it gets going."

"'tis down for the night, Maureen. Still, it means it will be nice and quiet for us, which is all to the good. What has you coming all the way out here anyway?" Mulholland said.

"I wanted to have a word about that Dalton woman. It seems that she was holding out on us when we were looking for her brother, and it caused us quite a delay. What do you think, Séan?"

Mulholland said nothing for a minute or two, and then Peadar Tobin came in with a tray bearing three big mugs of tea and a plate of chocolate digestive biscuits.

Mulholland took a sip of the hot drink and said, "I know what you mean, Maureen. But I don't think there's be a great deal of mileage in charging her. The DPP probably wouldn't go for it, and if she did have to appear in court, she'd win over the judge easily enough. And whatever about delay, she didn't actually make the situation any worse."

He studied Maureen Lyons' face for a reaction as he was speaking, and thought he could sense a softening in her expression.

"I suppose you're right, Séan. But I think you need to go and have a word all the same. We're not finished with McCarthy yet by any means, and she needs to know that she can't hide him away again. I'd take a very dim view if that was to happen."

Mulholland had the good sense to change tack while he was ahead.

"What about young Gerard anyway? What's the story there?"

"It looks as if he's been flogging data belonging to American companies out the back door to heaven knows who. You know when you get a phone call from someone with a foreign accent pretending to be from your bank asking for your account number and PIN? Well, that's where this data is going, it seems."

"God, that's shocking. And can you put him away for that?"

"It's not that simple, Séan. There's politicians and all sorts after getting involved now, and we have to tread very carefully. I've been told not to upset the applecart."

"Ah, 'tis always the same, Maureen. I don't know how you put up with it," Mulholland said.

"I don't usually, but there's a lot at stake here."

"Anyway, it's good that you got someone for that Lavelle killing. Yer one must have been in a right old state to bash his head in," Mulholland said.

"Unrequited love, Séan. The oldest motive in the book, and we couldn't see it for a long time. But, yes, it's good that it's sorted now."

"What will the lassie get, do you think?"

"I'd say she'll get away with manslaughter, so probably eight or ten. But she'll be out in five if things run true to form," Lyons said.

"Not much for a life, is it?"

"No, not much at all. Well, thanks for the tea, Séan. Always good to catch up with you. Can I leave the Dalton thing in your hands?"

"Sure, of course you can, and don't worry, she'll know which side her bread is buttered by the time I've finished with her. Are you staying out overnight, or will you head back?"

"No, I have to get back. There's still lots to be done with this whole mess yet. I'll give you a call in a day or two to bring you fully up to date."

"Aye, right you are. Thanks, Maureen."

Chapter Thirty-six

When Lyons got back to Salthill where she shared a house with Mick Hays, he was already at home. He had the fire lit, and the house was warm and cosy, a safe haven from the rain and wind battering the coast outside.

"Hi, Maureen," he said when she came into the kitchen. "Have you eaten?"

"I'm OK thanks, love. I'll get a sandwich or something in a while. I just need to unwind after the drive."

"OK. Can I tempt you to a glass of wine?"

"Yes, thanks, that would be lovely."

Hays went to the fridge and poured a generous measure of Lyons' favourite tipple and handed it to her. They sat down at the kitchen table.

"I need to run something by you, Mick," Lyons said.

"Oh-oh, sounds ominous."

"No, it's nothing bad. It's just I need your advice on my plan to tie off the loose ends in the Lavelle case. It's a bit tricky. I don't want to get my fingers burned."

"That's not like you, love. Why now?"

"Well, after that business with the Limerick job, and the intervention from Dublin on the Lavelle case, I want to stay squeaky clean for a while. Keep the head down, sort of thing."

"OK. So, what's your plan?"

Lyons outlined what she was proposing to deal with the fallout from the Lavelle killing. When she had finished, she said, "What do you think?"

"It's not without some risk, but then I think any course of action would likely be the same. I think it could probably work, but it will have to be done carefully and tactfully. Do you need my help?"

"No, I don't think so, unless it goes pear-shaped, then I'll need you to clean up the mess!"

"Terrific. I think I might leave town for a week or two! Joke!"

"I'll try not to screw it up, Mick, honest. Now, why have I got an empty glass in my hand?" she said, smiling.

* * *

The next morning, Sally Fahy drove out to the house where Ursula Kenny was staying, arriving at just before ten. The rain had blown through overnight, and while it had left behind some pretty serious puddles on the road, at least it had now stopped chucking it down, although it was still dull and quite cold.

Fahy knocked at the door, and after a few minutes, it was opened by Kenny herself.

"Oh, hello, Sergeant. Do you want to come in?"

"Yes, please, Ursula. How are you feeling?"

Kenny said nothing until they had walked down along the hallway into the kitchen at the back of the house. As she turned to sit down at the kitchen table, she said, "Pretty stupid, to be honest. Am I in more trouble?"

Fahy pulled out a chair and sat down.

"No, at least I don't think so. It kind of depends on what you tell me today. I need to know what's really been going on with GMC-IT out at the university. We know

McCarthy has been selling data to the Far East, but I need to know how the whole thing works and who is involved."

Kenny covered her face with her hands, and sighed heavily.

"Oh, gosh, where to start?"

"What about at the beginning?" Fahy said.

"OK. Well, you know that Gerard gets huge downloads of data every day from a number of companies in the USA. It's what we call raw data. It's all mixed up, with no rhyme or reason to it when he gets it. He then uses his special programs to analyse the data. This enables him to categorize it into data sets that are of interest to the company that sent it. For example, he gets purchasing history from a huge American supermarket to do with their loyalty club. He can analyse that data and break it down into blocks that are of special interest to companies targeting homeowners, or people who buy budget clothing lines. When he sends it back, the stores use this for promotion directly to the consumers, and also to inform their purchasing for in-store stocking. But he does something else too. He takes some of these records and partially anonymizes them, and then sells them on to companies in the Far East."

"Sorry, I don't understand. What does anonymize mean?"

"Sorry. He strips off some of the data like the customer's social security number, and part of the address. Sometimes he even blanks out the names. That way the data can't be traced back to him."

"And what do the people he sells that data do with it?"

"God only knows, but nothing good, that's for certain. They pay him in cryptocurrency so it can't be traced."

"I sec. And I assume that the US companies know nothing of this?"

"Of course not," Kenny said.

"So, where do you come in?"

"I submit the programs to run at night, and sort out any problems that arise. Sometimes the raw data isn't in the right format, and the programs stop working, so I clear down the system and restart it for him."

"Is that all?" Fahy said.

"No, no it's not. I also strip down the data that he sends away. We only take one in every hundred records or thereabouts, but there's so much of it, it doesn't matter."

"I see. And what do you get out of it?"

"He pays me. I don't earn much from the university. Gerard tops me up every month with a nice little bonus. Oh, and by the way, we are an item too. We go out together."

"How much do you get every month?" Fahy said.

"It varies, but it's usually around €1,000."

"Hmm… I see. This selling on the data must be very lucrative."

"Oh, it is. And you might as well know, he bungs Madden every month too. The college raises an invoice for the use of the computer, but Gerard pays Madden as well. And he gets more than I do."

"Why did you try to take your own life, Ursula?"

"I thought all this would come out and I'd be disgraced. And Gerard dumped me into the bargain. He said some pretty nasty things, so it wasn't worth going on."

"Nothing is worth that, Ursula. Believe me."

"I suppose I'll go to jail now then," Kenny said, tearing up.

"That's not up to us, Ursula. But this isn't as straightforward as it may appear. I'm not sure how it is all going to work out, but I wouldn't pack your overnight bag just yet," Fahy said, smiling.

"What happens now then?"

"You'll have to come in and make a formal statement about all of this. Then it's up to the bosses to take it on. But I can't stress enough that you keep all of this to yourself for now. Don't breathe a word of it to anyone. Got it?"

"Yes, OK. When do you want me to come in?" Kenny said.

"This afternoon or tomorrow would be good. When are you due back at work?"

"They told me to take a week off. But I'm not sure I want to go back there at all, to be honest. I'd get another job as a computer operator quite easily without all this nonsense."

"It might be best. But let's see how it all pans out. When you come into the station, ask for me, and I'll show you the ropes."

"OK. And thanks, Sergeant."

"For what?"

"For not bawling me out for being a silly cow."

Fahy just smiled, got up and left.

Chapter Thirty-seven

When Lyons arrived in Mill Street the following morning, she brought her crew together. When they had equipped themselves with the almost mandatory cups of tea and coffee, she addressed the little group.

"Right, folks. Here's the plan. I'd like Eamon to go out to the university and bring Professor Madden in. Don't say what it's about, and don't arrest him or anything. Just say that your boss is inviting him in for a chat, and make it clear, very subtly, that it would be unwise for him to decline. But I don't want a big scene. Take an unmarked car too. Can you handle that?"

"Yes, sure. No problem. What do I do when I have him here?"

"Just keep him entertained till the others arrive."

"Who are the others?" Flynn said.

"Ursula Kenny and Gerard McCarthy. Kenny is coming in this morning in any case. Sally, you can look after that. Make sure she's here when Eamon gets back with the professor. I'll go and get McCarthy, and then all six of us are going to have a nice little powwow. And hopefully, that will put the whole thing to bed nicely. I've already squared Séan Mulholland off with regard to

Christine Dalton. OK. Let's get to it. I'll ask John to get a nice comfortable room upstairs for the discussion. We don't want to treat them like criminals."

"But surely, that's just what they are, boss?" Flynn said.

"Maybe, Eamon, but this whole thing is a lot bigger than we think. If the likes of Amazon, Microsoft, Intel, Apple, HP, Dell and all the other US companies that Ireland depends on for tax revenue get spooked about the integrity of their operations here, it could have very serious consequences. Panic could run through them like a bush fire, and no one would be well served by that. So, it's a case of softly-softly, and I have that from the highest authority in the land by the way."

"Cripes. Is it that serious, boss?" Fahy said.

"Yes, it is. So now you can see the need for absolute discretion and complete secrecy about all of this. There's to be no pub talk about it or any other leaks. This is serious shit. Agreed, everyone?"

They all acknowledged Lyons' request.

* * *

By mid-morning, Madden, Kenny and McCarthy had been collected and were being entertained, if that's what you could call it, in one of the large and quite plush offices on the top floor of the building. They had been furnished with refreshments, and were quite relaxed, if a little curious as to the purpose of their visit.

Lyons came in with her two colleagues, and made the introductions all around.

"Thank you all for coming in this morning. I'm sure you are wondering exactly why we have asked you to be here, so I'm going to get straight to the point," Lyons said. She looked at the assembled group to ensure that she had their full attention.

"We have, thankfully, arrested someone for the killing of Jack Lavelle out at Kingstown on Christmas Eve last, so as far as the Gardaí are concerned, that matter is now closed," she went on.

Professor Madden spoke before she could continue.

"Sorry, Inspector, but I can't imagine why you think that could possibly have any relevance for me."

"All in good time, Professor. Let me explain," Lyons said.

The academic remained silent, though he still had a somewhat perplexed look about him.

Lyons continued.

"We know about the business that GMC-IT is using the college computers for, and we know about the little extra that Mr McCarthy earns from his illegal sale of his clients' data as well. And we know that you are all in receipt of payment as you are all complicit in this activity."

Here Lyons paused for effect, as Kenny, McCarthy and Madden all looked at each other.

"However, while normally I would be all in favour of prosecuting this illegal activity to the fullest extent of the law, it has been pointed out to me that such a course of action would not be in the national interests. But that doesn't mean you lot are off the hook, and it doesn't mean that this can continue." She paused again to let what she had just said sink in.

"What I am now going to propose must not be uttered beyond this room. If what I am going to suggest leaks, then you can all expect very serious consequences which would almost certainly involve custodial sentences for each of you."

Madden interjected again.

"What exactly do you propose, Inspector?"

"You, Professor Madden, will apply to the university for early retirement on health grounds. You can remain in post till the end of this academic year if you wish, but not beyond that time. As for you, Mr McCarthy, you will continue to process data in accordance with your contracts with the American companies until those contracts expire, and you will not renew them. Our information is that most of these contracts have less than a year to run. You will, of course, cease the practice of sidelining data to the Far East at once. Miss Kenny, you have already expressed an interest in changing jobs, and that is a course of action we would like you to pursue without delay. And just in case you think that you can just carry on regardless and completely ignore my proposal, be advised that all of this activity on the university's computer system is now being monitored. For the moment that is being done from here, but it may be passed over to the Irish Data Protection Commission at some later date if we so choose. Have you any questions?"

The group remained silent for a few moments of contemplation. Then Gerard McCarthy asked, "What if we don't go along with your proposal?"

"That, Mr McCarthy, would be most unwise. As I have said, should any of this get out – even as a rumour – then the full weight of the law will be brought down heavily upon you all. We would have to do that in order to try and protect Ireland's excellent reputation with foreign investors. I have made arrangements here to see that all of this stays under wraps, but only on the conditions I have outlined. So, I'll now ask for your agreement to my proposal, and when you have given it, you are free to go to put the wheels in motion."

Madden, Kenny and McCarthy looked at each other, but Ursula Kenny was the first to speak.

"Fine by me. I'm done with the university anyway, and I'm done with you, too, Gerard. I'll probably move to Dublin or London, so you can take this as my official notice," she said, looking defiantly at Madden.

Lyons turned her attention to Gerard McCarthy. "What about you, Mr McCarthy?"

"Will my sister be in trouble over any of this?" he said.

"No. That matter has been dealt with separately, as I said at the outset. So, do I have your agreement?"

"Yes, yes, of course. You are right. My contracts with the Americans are all reasonably short term. I'll just not renew them when they're up at the end of the year."

Lyons then addressed Madden. "What about you, Professor?"

"Well, I'm in quite good health as it happens. But I've always been a bit uneasy about what we got involved in. I managed to persuade myself that no one was being disadvantaged by what was being done, but I know that's not really true. For the sake of the others, I'll go along with what you have requested. I'm a keen golfer, and I can spend more time on the greens, and my wife won't be displeased."

"Excellent. Then we are all in agreement about the best way to proceed. If there are no more questions, then let's leave it at that," Lyons said.

* * *

When the three conspirators had left the Garda station, Flynn, Fahy and Lyons gathered in Lyons' office.

"That was brilliant, boss," Flynn said, "do you think they'll stick to their part of the bargain?"

"I do. And I have taken out some insurance to make sure that they do. We have a little side-hustle of our own going on. Tell Eamon, Sally," Lyons said.

"When I was with Ursula, I did a little negotiation with her as part of the deal for letting her off the hook," Fahy said. "She gave me one of the college's encoded laptops, which is now in the very capable hands of one John O'Connor. She told me how to use the gateway into the college's mainframe to monitor McCarthy's data. John will be able to see if there's any more data being shipped out east."

"Blimey," Flynn said, "you're a dark horse all the same, boss."

"Sometimes, you have to set a thief to catch a thief, Eamon!"

Epilogue

When Ursula Kenny moved from Galway to London to take up a new position as a computer operator at King's College London at their Guy's Campus, it was the first indication that the trio would be following through on their undertaking to the Galway Gardaí.

She had hooked up with an old school friend who had preceded her to the capital of the United Kingdom, and the two women rented a small flat not far from London Bridge. Over time, Kenny put the events of that fateful Christmas behind her, and some two years later, she started going out with a colleague from KCL, and a few months after that, she became engaged and married her fiancé. They moved out of town to a bigger apartment in Finchley, North London, and when last heard of had started a family.

Sandra Ward fared less well. She was brought before the court in Galway. The director of public prosecutions determined that a charge of murder would be difficult to prove, and there was little to show that Ward had set out with the intention of killing her friend. She pleaded guilty to the lesser charge of manslaughter, and was given a sentence of nine years, with the last two years suspended on the basis of her guilty plea. In the event, she served just five years, and when released, she moved to Dublin, where she got a new job as an interior designer with one of the large department stores.

Professor Rían Madden tendered his resignation to the university shortly after the meeting with the detectives in Galway. His resignation on health grounds raised a few eyebrows at the college, but it wasn't questioned extensively, and at the end of the summer term he left his role permanently. He now plays golf a few times a week, and he donated much of his ill-gotten gains to medical research at the university to salve his conscience.

Gerard McCarthy's business started to flounder later that same year. When he didn't renew the contracts with the American companies, there was nothing left of it. He tried for a while to find alternative sources of work, but by the middle of the following year, he had run out of funds and ideas, and he filed for voluntary liquidation. His property out at Kingstown had progressed to the erection of exterior walls, but had got no further due to his lack of ability to finance it. His mobile home lies deserted, slowly decaying at the mercy of the strong westerly winds blowing in from the Atlantic Ocean. When his company folded, he took a job with a large online bookmaker in the United Kingdom as a data analyst, and remains in that job to this day, working for a decent wage.

Séan Mulholland visited Christine Dalton a few times in the months following the discovery of Jack Lavelle's body at her brother's building site at Kingstown. They had some candid conversations about the obstruction of justice, and Mulholland, in his own gentle style, demonstrated the error of her ways to her. He was persuaded of her remorse in the matter, and things went no further.

Superintendent Plunkett was pleased that the whole matter had been put to bed without any significant exposure of the fiddle that had been going on. His bosses in Dublin were satisfied that any kind of political crisis had been averted, and although nothing was said overtly, Plunkett received an acknowledgement of his diplomacy from his political masters. He relayed his appreciation on, down the ranks, and during a meeting with Hays a few weeks after things had died down, he congratulated himself on his judgement in keeping Maureen Lyons in Galway. When Hays told Lyons about this, she was unimpressed, but inwardly she, too, was delighted that she hadn't been pushed to move to Limerick.

List of Characters

Detective Superintendent Mick Hays – in overall charge of the detectives at Mill Street Garda station.

Superintendent Finbarr Plunkett – a wily senior officer who tries to keep everyone happy.

Senior Inspector Maureen Lyons – a feisty detective with a strong track record for solving crime in Galway.

Inspector Eamon Flynn – a tenacious detective who follows a line of enquiry to the very end.

Detective Sally Fahy – a pretty young officer who is a lot tougher than she looks.

Séan Mulholland – runs the Clifden Garda station with traditional methods, but his experience ensures that he gets results.

Garda Jim Dolan – Séan Mulholland's right-hand man.

Angela Dolan – Jim Dolan's wife.

Garda Peadar Tobin – another member of the Clifden police team.

Garda Pascal Brosnan – runs the Roundstone Garda station.

Garda Mary Fallon – Pascal Brosnan's helper in Roundstone.

Garda John O'Connor – a nerdy uniformed officer who loves tinkering with technology.

Dr Julian Dodd – an excellent pathologist with a dry sense of humour.

Sinéad Loughran – a good-humoured forensic officer.

Christine Dalton – lives in a remote area near Clifden.

Gerard McCarthy – a graduate of UCG, now a businessman, but too clever for his own good.

Tadgh Deasy – runs a rather run-down garage near Roundstone.

Ursula Kenny – a computer operator with a poor choice in men.

Jack Lavelle – a graduate of UCG who has run out of luck.

Professor Rían Madden – a university don nearing retirement.

Sandra Ward – an interior designer with a furious temper.

If you enjoyed this book, please let others know by leaving a quick review on Amazon. Also, if you spot anything untoward in the paperback, get in touch. We strive for the best quality and appreciate reader feedback.

editor@thebookfolks.com

www.thebookfolks.com

MORE BOOKS BY DAVID PEARSON

In this series:

Murder on the Old Bog Road (Book 1)
Murder at the Old Cottage (Book 2)
Murder on the West Coast (Book 3)
Murder at the Pony Show (Book 4)
Murder on Pay Day (Book 5)
Murder in the Air (Book 6)
Murder at the Holiday Home (Book 7)
Murder on the Peninsula (Book 8)
Murder at the Races (Book 9)
Murder in a Safe Haven (Book 10)
Murder in an Irish Bog (Book 11)
Murder in a Seaside Town (Book 12)
Murder by the Hidden Bay (Book 13)
Murder at the Arts Festival (Book 14)

In the Dublin Homicides Series:

A Deadly Dividend
A Fatal Liaison
The China Chapter
Lethal in Small Doses
Plane Dead
Passion for Murder

If you have enjoyed David Pearson's Galway Homicides series, check out his series of murder mysteries set in Dublin.

Two very different police officers work together to solve cases in this Irish mystery series with a cozy feel.

For Detective Inspector Aidan Burke, policing Dublin's streets is a duty, but protecting his officers comes first. That provides a good environment for promising detectives like DS Fiona Moore to grow. As this series of murder mysteries set in the metropolitan but at times parochial city and its surroundings progresses, we see Moore tackle difficult and dangerous cases with a good success rate. As Burke himself rises in rank, they become a formidable crime fighting duo.

OTHER TITLES OF INTEREST

THE MYSTERY OF THE HIDDEN FORTUNE
by Christine McHaines

Quentin Cadbury, a useless twenty-something, is left to look after his late aunt's London house when his parents head to Australia. But burglars seem determined to break in, and not even the stray cat he befriends can help him. As the thieves are after something pretty valuable, and illegal, he must grow up pretty fast to get out of a sticky situation.

THE PIPER'S CHILDREN by Iain Henn

The first standalone book in a new series of mysteries set in the US

A boy is found wandering in the woods, dressed in medieval clothes and speaking a strange language. When another child turns up, it doesn't shed any more light on the mystery for FBI agent Ilona Farris. Only by digging into her own past will she begin to work out what is going on, and who these children are, seemingly lost in time.

All our books are FREE with Kindle Unlimited and available in paperback.

www.thebookfolks.com

Printed in Great Britain
by Amazon

41746344R00121